Caroline Vermalle is a former BBC producer and the prize-winning author of seven novels. Having travelled the world with her family and built a wooden house in a forest, she now lives between a small seaside town in Vendée (France) and a small seaside town in the Eastern Cape (South Africa) with her son, a black cat and her husband, South African architect-turned-author Ryan von Ruben.

Anna Aitken studied French and German at St Peter's College, Oxford. She has co-translated two novels by Guillaume Musso. She currently lives and works in London.

George's Grand Tour

George's Grand Tour

Caroline Vermalle

Translated from the French by Anna Aitken

Gallic Books
London

This book is supported by the Institut français du Royaume-Uni as part of the Burgess programme.
www.frenchbooknews.com

A Gallic Book

First published in France as *L'avant-dernière chance*
by Editions Calmann-Lévy, 2009

First published in Great Britain in 2015 by Gallic Books,
59 Ebury Street, London, SW1W 0NZ

A CIP record for this book is available from the British Library
ISBN 978-1-908313-73-7

Typeset in Fournier MT by Gallic Books
Printed and bound by CPI Group (UK) Ltd, Croydon, CR0 4YY

2 4 6 8 10 9 7 5 3 1

To Christiane and André,
in memory of Ninette and Marcel, my grandparents.

Tuesday 21 October

London

Adèle was jolted from extreme boredom by the gentle buzzing of her phone. Mobile phones were to be kept switched off at all times, she had been told often enough. But she had been careful to put it on vibrate and anyway, today was her twenty-third birthday and she was waiting to see how many of her friends were going to remember. The numbers had been disappointing so far. Every now and again she would check to see if anyone was watching before quickly glancing at the screen, which was just poking out of the top of her jeans. She would have to wait for the right moment to read this new message and that moment was not now, seeing as the inspector in the room next door was calling it murder.

She was perched awkwardly on a crate in the long dark corridor that led to the bedroom. The only sounds were from the street below – a scooter, a lorry, a dog, the distant wail of a siren. She glanced into the bedroom where dust swirled under a spotlight. There was a beautifully carved, dark wooden four-poster bed, a quilt falling in mounds of pink satin, and the deceased, who was wearing a pair of forties-style pyjamas. His face was grey, and he had the tragic air of a murder victim about him. For this was a case of murder, the inspector was sure of it, so sure in fact that he had repeated it three times over. The man's daily injection of insulin had been swapped for eye drops; the little bottles were there to prove it. The eighty-three-year-old victim had left his family a colossal fortune, along with the London mansion they all called home. Every time the inspector said the word 'crime', the granddaughter would break down in tears and her fiancé would try to console her. But it was no use. The young woman was kneeling by the bed with her face buried in the quilt, clasping the hands of the corpse and muttering words that could barely be made out through her almost absurdly loud sobs. She poured out her grief, childhood memories and most of all regrets, of which there appeared to be many; no wonder, since she was now listing them for the fourth time. A very dignified elderly lady was standing upright next to the bed, nodding her head in time to the regrets that the young girl was counting off like rosary beads. This woman was the great-aunt, the sister-in-law of the deceased. There were others waiting behind the door who remained silent. The inspector said it again: the killer was one of the family members. It was no time to be checking one's text messages.

This was not Adèle's first murder scene. They bored her immensely, and she had fallen into a daydream as she waited for this one to finish. Just before her phone had vibrated, it had occurred to her that she and the young woman crying in the bedroom looked alike. Same age, same long, thick brown hair, same slim figure. But, without necessarily being prettier, the girl in the bedroom was better dressed, more polished; her hands were soft and she was obviously used to drawing gazes. Adèle, by contrast, was more of a tomboy, in spite of her delicate features. What was more, she was not rich, and nobody ever paid any attention to her. Even on her birthday. On the other hand, she thought that the dead man wasn't half as stylish as Irving Ferns. Irving Ferns. She felt a pang in her chest at the thought of him.

The suspense was unbearable – who had sent her the text? The young lawyer she had met at a party a month ago? But how could he have known it was her birthday today? She looked around her. The corridor was crowded, there were about thirty people crammed into the narrow space, all standing still, trying hard not to make the floor creak. Some were scratching their noses, some biting their nails. People mimed at each other because even whispering was frowned upon. But no one seemed to take any notice of Adèle. She checked one last time that the silence police weren't in the corridor – no, they were busy with the corpse – got out her mobile and opened the text message she had just received.

She had to peer closely at the screen to be sure that she had read it right, and couldn't stop herself from letting out a muffled cry of surprise, dropping the phone as she did. It crashed onto the parquet floor of the old house with a deafening clatter. Everyone jumped and turned to look at Adèle. A second later, an angry voice shouted from the bedroom.

'CUT! CUT! What's going on out there, for God's sake?' And the first assistant director burst into the corridor.

Adèle mumbled, 'I'm so sorry, John, I … '

The entire crew was now staring at Adèle, actors included. Then, in a matter of seconds, their attention turned to something else. This kind of thing happened a lot, and it gave everyone the chance of a breather.

John shouted to the group, 'Come on, let's concentrate. We're almost done. There's champagne waiting for us, guys! So come on, one last push, chaps.' The director took the opportunity to give the actors some more instructions, the dead man was able to rub his eyes and share a joke with the elderly aunt, the director of photography adjusted the lighting and the fifth take was ready to begin.

This was the last day of shooting. They were filming an adaptation of Agatha Christie's *Crooked House* for British television. The first chapter, in which the corpse was discovered, had already been filmed on the first day of shooting a month earlier, but they had had to reshoot it. It was the last scene to film and, everyone hoped, the last take. Afterwards there would be a big party to celebrate.

'Silence, silence please … Camera. Action.'

Adèle had not moved from her crate. Her mobile phone was still clenched in her hand. For once, she was grateful for the silence. On top of the commotion caused by her dropping her phone, she was still in shock from the text itself. Finally, she worked up the courage to loosen her fingers and look down at the screen.

Hpy Bday Adl, luv frm ur granpa.
(Happy Birthday Adèle, love from your grandpa.)

She managed to keep herself from crying, but couldn't hold back the smile that suddenly lit up her face and spread a warm glow through her chest. Because this silly, slightly awkward text that was trying to sound young was something truly special. Poetic even, and so touching. As well as totally impossible, of course.

There are things in life that are meant to be kept private. And others that are to be shared with all and sundry. This text belonged to the latter category. This was a story that had to be told, and Adèle felt restless and full of emotion.

It was decided that the scene would be shot a sixth time. But Adèle was no longer paying attention to the filming. She was thinking about her story. It was not a particularly long story but it had to be told in full in order to convey what was so extraordinary about this text message. Yes, she had to start from the beginning, one month earlier, 18 September. A month was not a long time, yet in that time hearts had opened, suitcases had shut, and tears had fallen where they were no longer expected. And as a drama played out for the sixth time in the other room, Adèle used these last moments of silence as a chance to remember.

In the dimly lit corridor, she replayed the events of the last month in her head, events that had changed her life in a small way, but which had changed the lives of others beyond measure.

Thursday 18 September

Chanteloup (Deux-Sèvres)

After about ten rings there was finally an answer.

'Hello?' said a slightly shaky voice.

'Hi Grandpa, it's Adèle.'

'Hello?' repeated the old man.

'Grandpa?'

'Yes?'

'It's Adèle!'

'Oh, hello, sweetheart. How are you?'

'Oh, fine, and you?'

'Oh, you know, I'm …' he replied with unmistakable weariness. 'Why are you calling?'

'Well … Mum explained that she's going travelling, didn't she?'

'Yes, in Peru, she told me.'

'OK, good, well I just wanted you to know that you can call me if there are any problems. I can come and see you.'

'Oh right.'

'While she's away, I mean, you can call me,' Adèle kept on, a little disappointed by her grandfather's lack of enthusiasm.

'Okey doke, that's good,' he replied politely.

'And you've got my number, Grandpa?'

'Yes, your mother gave it to me. But Adèle, are you still living in London, dear?'

'Yes, but don't worry, it's not that far. I can get the train to you, it wouldn't take long,' Adèle lied.

'Oh yes, you just get the train to Poitiers and then the bus, don't you?'

'Exactly,' said Adèle, who had no idea how to get there, having not visited him for almost ten years.

'And how long would the journey be overall?'

'Oh, I don't know, half a day, maybe a little more,' guessed Adèle. But she suspected it would take a lot longer than that. Her grandfather lived in a hamlet near Chanteloup, a minuscule village tucked away in the forest in Deux-Sèvres.

'Jolly good. But there's no need anyway. Right, lots of love, bye.'

'Wait, Grandpa, do you still have the phone that Mum gave you?'

'Oh, you know, mobile phones ...' said her grandfather, who considered cutting-edge technology to be a lot of old nonsense. But luckily for Adèle, he would tolerate phone conversations on the condition that they were kept very short and were limited to the bare essentials. And a rant about progress did not, for today at least, count as essential.

'But you still have it, right?' Adèle persisted.

'Yes, yes.'

'Good, well, keep it with you and call if you need anything.'

'Oh, I don't need anything. Right, goodbye, sweetheart.' And with that he hung up.

No, of course he didn't need anything. His heart hadn't been right since a heart attack in 1995, he had a pacemaker in his chest, a knee that threatened to go at any moment, and a pair of lungs that had been thoroughly blackened by forty years of Gitanes ... But he went about his life as he always had, ate like a horse, tended his garden, whistled as he did the dishes. And he still had enough fight in him to fire swear words at his doctors, who regularly predicted he had only a few months left in him. They had said the same for almost fifteen years. Well, that was the story according to Françoise, Adèle's mother; Adèle herself had very little contact with him. And this was no cause for guilt, since he repeated incessantly, with the delicacy and restraint he was known for, that he just wanted to be 'left the hell alone'.

Adèle put her mobile phone into the pocket of her combat trousers. 7.23 p.m. She had been standing there waiting in the middle of the street for at least a quarter of an hour. The September evening air was still warm, and Brick Lane was filled with the sound of drunken laughter coming from the overcrowded Swan pub. Adèle had never liked this part of town, even if her friends assured her that it was the coolest place in London. On rare sunny days, she appreciated its vibrant colours and found the odd gem in its unusual shops. But on grey days, her senses were overloaded with the smells of curry spices, the rubbish everywhere, the waiters hawking outside the Indian restaurants and the dark, dirty buildings. And yet over the next month, she was going to have to spend many long days and even some nights in this area. For here, on a road with a bilingual English and Bengali street sign, was the one and only filming location: a three-storey house built of stone as grey as the English sky. The house was barely noticeable amongst the old warehouses lining the gloomy little street whose most regular visitors were junkies and groups of drunken girls. Adèle was standing by the front door. Inside, things were already getting started. 7.27 p.m. Her working day was just beginning, and it had not got off to a good start.

She pulled the staff memo from her pocket and read it over for the third time. The leading actor was expected in make-up at 7.30. Her name – Adèle Montsouris – was written next to his. It was funny to see their two names side by side, as they were at opposite ends of the television-industry food chain. He was a star of BBC period dramas with a salary of several hundred thousand pounds, and she was right at the bottom, twenty-two years old and a runner, unpaid of course; she was doing it 'for the experience'. She fetched teas and coffees, booked taxis and babysat actors of all ages. She was the first to arrive on set and the last to leave. This was all the 'experience' Adèle had managed to accumulate over the course of three films, and without being paid a penny for her trouble. The fact that her name was next to his meant that if he was late, the first, second, second-second and third assistant directors were entitled to hold her responsible – and people loved to shout at each other on film sets. So she in turn would have to shout at the taxi driver, find a plan B, warn the make-up artist and all the rest of it. The third day of shooting had barely begun and Adèle could already feel her muscles tensing in anticipation of this new disaster. Since the trials of the preceding days were also weighing on her mind, Adèle soon forgot the distant grandfather she had just spoken to.

But he had not forgotten her. Her phone call had turned everything, *everything* upside down.

George Nicoleau stayed by the phone in the corridor for some time, utterly perplexed.

'Dammit,' he said to himself aloud. 'Dammit, dammit, and dammit again. Damn!'

Not that he didn't appreciate that Adèle had got in touch – no indeed, her call had boosted him in some way, and he had been feeling a little deflated that evening. His granddaughter had not come to visit him since her parents' divorce, which must have been, what, almost ten years ago. She had sent him a card every year wishing him a happy new year, and there had been a few postcards when she first moved to London. There they all were, in fact, tacked to the faded wallpaper, next to the 2008 Postal Services calendar, above the telephone table. He had been delighted to receive them, and they had made Arlette happy as well. Arlette … She had particularly liked that one there, the one with Big Ben in black and white. She had thought it artistic. Well, the novelty value of London must have worn off quickly because the postcards had stopped coming, and phone calls were few and far between. This evening's call might have made him happy in one respect, but it had still saddled him with one heck of a problem.

All the plans he and Charles had made together might come to diddly-squat. He had to fill in his accomplice, tonight if possible.

Luckily it was not Wednesday or Saturday, so Charles was probably going to come round for tea in time for the weather report.

George went back into the living room, choosing his path carefully as he had always done. His tall, now slightly stooped frame just about fit under the beams of the cottage. These beams had been getting in his way since he was a teenager, but one advantage of getting older was that he no longer banged his head against the ceiling. Old age had arrived rather unexpectedly, because in his head he felt as young as ever and for an old fogey of eighty-three, he didn't think he was in too bad a shape, should the question cross his mind. For starters, he still had a thick mop of hair poking out from under his baseball cap. Not quite the mane he had once boasted, but all things considered, he thought his hair had held out very well. Then there were his jeans and Reeboks – worn for comfort, of course, rather than out of a desire to be fashionable, something he regarded with great disdain. And most importantly, when it came to his memory not only was he second to none at the old folks' club, he could also give any youngster in the village a run for their money. Admittedly his heart had been a little fragile since the operation. But as with his knee, his bladder and his back, he just had to follow the instruction manual, take the right medication and the rest would take care of itself.

George lowered himself into his chair, an old plastic sun lounger piled with various cushions. It was not that he couldn't afford a proper armchair. Monsieur Nicoleau was not short of cash – in fact he had more of it than he knew what to do with. It wasn't the butchery he had run for forty years that had made his fortune, though it had been quite a successful little business. George Nicoleau had always invested in land and property, bought and sold at as good a time as any, and above all, lived frugally and saved regularly. He was positively rolling in it. But he had never found an armchair as comfortable as this one.

He started to consider the problem and, in order to gather his thoughts, reached for the remote control lying on top of the latest edition of *TéléStar* and switched on the TV. He had missed the serious news at eight o'clock; now, half an hour later, they had moved on to the lighter stuff. He tended to prefer these items to the headlines, which came from a world he no longer recognised. His thoughts turned to Adèle again. He looked over at the suitcase that stood by the living-room door. They were due to set off exactly a week from now. His modest suitcase had been packed for two days. He had bought it – he now remembered – in Biarritz in 1985. The year Adèle was born, in fact. He had briefly considered investing in a new one for the occasion, a modern one with wheels. It would certainly have been more practical, but he was not planning on walking very far with it. It would have been a bit of a waste anyway; this one had barely been used. And as he was not taking any souvenirs from home with him, perhaps the suitcase itself would serve as a kind of memento.

He was distracted from these thoughts by the jingle that announced the weather report. At precisely the same moment, he heard the familiar sound of Charles's footsteps coming from the garage. George's house had a lovely front door bordered by flowers and a rock garden, and even a little garden gnome. But ever since they had first become neighbours thirty years ago, Charles had *always* come in through the cluttered garage, picking his way, despite his bad hip, through the cardboard boxes, rakes, buckets and other assorted odds and ends that lined the walls, and in some places were piled up to the ceiling. That was just the way it was.

Charles walked in, his eyes fixed on the television, and in a gesture that had been repeated every time he had walked in here for the last thirty years, he held his hand out to George. George shook it without taking his eyes off the screen. The weather forecaster was waving her arms in front of a sun-studded map of France.

'Oh, would you look at that! No rain tomorrow either!' cried Charles, who had not worked as a farmer for several years now (unless a handful of chickens in the garden and his great-granddaughter's pony in the old stables counted as farming) but had retained a healthy suspicion of dry weather.

'It looks like beautiful weather all the way, and not too hot either, would you believe.'

'You're right. Except for Pau, it's not looking so good down there. Still, plenty of time for that to change. We're not there yet, are we?'

Charles went to fetch two mugs from the old dresser.

'Stupid damned thing,' he said, massaging his hip. That hip was giving him a lot of bother these days, and yet, George thought to himself, Charles was still young, barely seventy-six. He was short and stocky with a round, bald head, rosy farmer's cheeks and large hands that had seen much hard labour. He wore sixties-style glasses and had the air of an honest man you could count on. And it was true: you could always count on Charles Lepensier.

George was reluctant to bring up Adèle. But he eventually took the plunge.

'That's just it, Charles. We're not there yet. I don't even know if we'll ever get there. We've got a problem. You remember Adèle, my granddaughter who lives over in London? She called this evening.'

Of course Charles remembered Adèle. George only had one granddaughter and no grandson so there was no risk of confusing her with anyone else. When it came to his own extended tribe, on the other hand, he was always getting names mixed up. Thanks to the family tendency not to hang about with producing offspring, he could now count eighteen grandchildren and four great-grandchildren, and, God willing, there would be more to come.

'Oh, really? Is everything alright in London?' Charles asked anxiously.

'Oh yes, everything's fine, just fine. That's not the problem … She's *worried*,' George said emphatically.

'What do you mean, she's worried … about you? What, just today? What's she getting worried about you now for, all of a sudden?'

'Yes, I was a bit taken aback as well. But I reckon it's *her mother* who's worried. So she must have asked the kid to, you know, keep tabs on me.'

'Blast it. Your women don't half choose their moments.'

'You're not wrong about that.'

'She's not going to come here though, is she?'

'Oh no, that wouldn't be like her. And even if she did decide to, I worked it out: it would take her at least thirteen hours to get here from London. No, what's really bothering me is that she'll call, you can bet on that. Probably not every day or anything, but it wouldn't surprise me if her mother had asked her to call once a week. Think about it, if I don't pick up the phone once or twice, all hell will break loose, and Françoise will come haring back from her Peruvian mountains. Just imagine what'll happen if they can't get hold of me for almost two months!'

'We should have seen this coming,' growled Charles, barely concealing his annoyance. 'It was too good to be true that your daughter decided to disappear off to the middle of nowhere for two months, no phone calls or anything. I could barely believe it, to be quite honest. I guess we just forgot she had *her* daughter up her sleeve.'

They had spent many hours discussing George's only daughter, Françoise. The woman who, since her divorce and the death of her mother five years earlier, had not let her father alone even for a moment, the woman who – rightly or wrongly – believed her father to be seriously ill, had suddenly decided to fly off to the depths of the Andes to take part in an endurance expedition. This in itself was not surprising as she was always signing up for marathons, treks and other such activities favoured by the moneyed classes. But on every trip, no matter the time difference, she would find a moment to call her father, every evening if she could. This time, however, she had promised two months of total radio silence. It was the chance they had been waiting for, and George and Charles had leapt at it. This was the moment to put their plan into action, or they never would. And now, with a week to go before their *grand départ*, they were back to square one.

George could feel himself being rapidly swept under a rising tide of dejection. If even Charles was losing faith in their plan, they were done for. The click of the kettle made Charles jump. He poured the tea in silence. Without looking up from the cups, he finally spoke.

'I know we've already talked about this but, George … are you sure you can't tell your daughter and granddaughter?'

'No, no, definitely not, let's not get into that again, for Pete's sake! If Françoise found out … you've seen what she's like, Charles. She'll put me straight into an old people's home where I'll get needles stuck in me every fifteen minutes and be escorted to the loo to take a piss, you can be sure of that. She'd have me preserved in formaldehyde if she could. She ought to be halfway up a mountain as we speak and she *promised* me, y'see, *promised* me, she drummed it into me that she wouldn't be able to call me *at all* for two months. So that's that, and so much the better. Now Adèle, being the clever girl that she is … we mustn't fool ourselves, she'll find a way. And then, and then, with a couple of clicks on the internet, bam! I'll find myself with a squadron of nurses on my tail. No, Françoise can't find out about this, not from me, not from you, not from Adèle. And that's that. Pass the tea.'

He lifted the cup to his lips and put it down again before continuing his rant.

'You see, for you, it's simple. None of this bothers your wife at all. She even encouraged you to do it, to go off for two months. I've got to tell you, Thérèse really surprised me there. Ah, Charles, I suppose we've only got ourselves to blame for the way our kids turn out!'

Charles smiled, but he looked deflated. The two men drank

their tea in silence. The ticking of the clock became almost deafening in their ears. George was the first to speak.

'Come on, show me what you've got.'

Shyly, like a child who had just been told off, Charles pulled out his leather satchel and retrieved the printouts and travel guides, spreading them over the wipe-clean tablecloth.

'What's all this, then?' asked George. 'Ah yes, of course, Sauveterre-de-Comminges, between Lannemezan and Foix. Stage eleven, that's a good one, that.'

These were the undisputed highlights of the evening visits, when the tea-drinking ritual was enlivened with a sense of adventure. Poring over the guidebooks and running their fingers over the dog-eared atlas, the two men sat surrounded by hotel reservations and colourful brochures, going over their route again and again, suddenly feeling thirty years younger. In seven days, they would embark on the Tour de France.

Friday 19 September

Chanteloup (Deux-Sèvres)

'The Tour de France?' exclaimed the young postman, somewhat taken aback.

'That's right,' George replied proudly.

'Blimey ... But, um ... you know ... with your bad knee and everything, isn't that going to be a bit, um, you know, a bit of a challenge?'

'What makes you think that? Our feet are barely going to touch the ground!'

'Well, exactly! That's what's worrying me! Three thousand five hundred kilometres on a bike, that takes some muscle!'

'Oh, no, no, no ... We're doing it by car,' replied George, disappointed that he had to correct this rather appealing misunderstanding so quickly.

'Oh, I see! Gosh, you really scared me there!' said the postman, laughing. 'I get it now. You had me worried there for a moment. There was I thinking—'

'Well, it's still going to be a long trip. Twenty-one stages and forty-nine villages. It's going to take us about two months, all in all.'

'Yeah, but, well, it's not like doing it on a bike, is it?' The young postman seemed to have lost interest now and he was just about to change the subject when George said:

'Yes, but even so, I can assure you it's taken a hell of a lot of organising. See, me and Charles, we've been working on this for months. He's been on the internet and everything.'

'Oh right,' said the postman politely. 'Well in that case, let me know what you want me to do with your post.'

There was no point pushing it. It was not the first time this had happened. He could have explained that they would be going to far-flung places, some of them dangerous, or even downright foreign (Italy!). He had sometimes found himself regretting that they were not in fact going by bike, just to see the look on people's faces. It got him down when people seemed to think his grand plan was worth peanuts. After all, even in a car it was still three thousand five hundred kilometres.

George sighed and got out his old orange notebook.

'Yes, right, you can give my mail to Thérèse ... from the twenty-fifth, so this coming Thursday until ... wait, let me see ... until 24 November. That's a Monday. If we end up taking longer, Thérèse will tell you, alright? Well, you'll work it out with her.'

'Great, I'll do that then. And the same with parcels? Oh that reminds me, one came for you earlier. Here you go.' He held out a small package about the size of a shoebox that was covered in what looked like home-made wrapping paper. George had been waiting for this for quite some time; it had not been easy to come by.

He went home and put the package into his suitcase without opening it. He had even left a space for it. Just as he was closing his rather sad little case, he was overcome by the absurdity of the whole project. It now seemed ridiculous, far-fetched and pointless. He returned to his armchair, wedged a few cushions behind his back, picked up the remote control and switched on the television. As he had done every lunchtime for years. It was just so easy to stick to a familiar routine. And here he was getting ready to start the Tour de France. Madness.

Why had he agreed to go with Charles? He of all people, who had so rarely left the *bocage*, even when he had been in the peak of good health. Why, at the age of eighty-three, had he suddenly caught the travel bug? His last chance, that was probably what everyone was saying. Go on, Grandpa, have one last go at it for your pride, buck yourself up and make yourself feel invincible one last time, pretend you're getting stronger, not weaker. 'Realising a boyhood dream at his age, isn't that great?' they'd say. Oh, he'd be lying if he said he didn't like the idea of getting people talking; he still had his pride, after all. But the whole thing made more sense for Charles, who was still young and healthy, relatively speaking, and had a large and happy family to boot. Things were so different for George. People were right, it was his last chance. It was his last chance to make a grand exit. It didn't even need to be dramatic, his exit. Just dignified. Standing.

His patched-up body was holding up, admittedly with a little discomfort, but holding up all the same. But the man inside had been in bad shape for a long time. Having more or less admitted defeat, he had sat back and waited for the doctors' prognoses to come true, for the statistics to be proved right and the odds to catch up with him. But they never did. So he had decided to go out and face the odds head on. Eighty-three years old, one set of aching limbs, three thousand five hundred kilometres and a two-month expedition. What it all added up to was so blindingly obvious that he had been surprised at Charles's insistence he go with him. And yet he had to complete this epic circuit, before the army of paramedics descended upon him to unleash an assault of well-intentioned humiliation and take every last freedom away from him.

But all this was by the by. These were all things he had told himself before, when he was still feeling brave. In those mad moments of enthusiasm, bravado and unbridled determination. But in the last few minutes, that had all gone out the window. Enthusiasm, determination and bravado had all deserted him. All that was left were the voices in his head. Those damned voices.

No, he wasn't losing the plot. The voices were of the common or garden variety. But this afternoon they really had him. They were the voices of his chair and the weather report, of his herbal tea and tomato plants, of all his familiar possessions and the house itself. They sang of the joys of everyday life, repeating a chorus we've all heard before: what's the use in change? The voices were telling him it would be easier to let fate come to him, to let it cradle him gently, oh so gently. To let the days run into one another, until his time was up. The voices were even whispering a ready-made excuse: this unexpected phone call.

The more George thought about their plan, the more he found it deeply, painfully ridiculous. This wasn't audacity, it was idiocy; not wisdom, but delusion. He looked at his suitcase sadly. It was neither Wednesday nor Saturday, so Charles would be coming over, and George would have to explain his change of heart. His knee was also playing up again, now that he came to think of it. And Charles would understand about that, what with his hip.

It was with a feeling of relief mixed with sadness that he turned his attention to the one o'clock news, and, avoiding the sight of his suitcase that was patiently waiting by the stove, he began to doze off. He had given in.

But on the other side of the garden, Charles had not given up. He was going to do this Tour de France, even if it meant dragging his friend along by the skin of his backside.

'The Tour de France? In a Runner Speedit?'

Little Lucas looked up at his grandfather, his round eyes filled with admiration.

'Granny, what's a Runner Speedit?'

'A Renault Scenic, Lucas. It's a car,' Thérèse answered calmly.

'Yes, but it's also got loads of gadgets inside it,' Charles added quickly.

'What gadgets, Grandpa?'

Charles was already regretting going down this rather slippery path. Discussing gadgets with a seven-year-old expert was a battle he was sure to lose.

'Lots of *options*, if you catch my drift.' There, that wasn't a bad response.

'And how many hours does it take?'

'Oh no, Lucas, we'll be doing our Tour de France over several weeks.'

'Oh. So you'll stop lots.'

'Yes, we're going to stop lots. Exactly,' Charles replied, disappointed.

They were all sitting in the kitchen, Charles and Thérèse, their granddaughter Annie and her husband Franck and their two children, Lucas and seven-month-old Justine. The little kitchen, whose wallpaper had probably been rather fashionable at one time, smelled of leeks and Mr Muscle. A little vase of dahlias from the garden stood on the Formica table. Photos of the grandchildren were tacked all over the walls, and strings of last year's tinsel were still hanging on the old grandfather clock. Everyone felt at home in this kitchen, especially Thérèse; this was her kingdom. Thérèse was small and round like a typical granny in a television show. She had no neck and small feet, neatly pressed blouses, bobbed grey hair worn with a brown clip, and an iron will. Charles and Thérèse had been married for fifty-nine years: they were happy and they knew it. Life had been kind to them, more or less, but the Lepensiers had learned to think positive long before the concept had become fashionable. Finding solutions to men's problems was Thérèse's area of expertise, and the women of the family had all inherited this talent.

Charles was now relying on his wife's ingenuity, as he had so many times before. It was unthinkable that they would abandon the project now. He and Thérèse had put all their hopes into it. And he couldn't do it alone, partly because George was financing the entire trip including the brand-new Renault Scenic, and partly because ... well, he just couldn't do it on his own.

'You know, Thérèse, we're not on the road yet. Even though we've been planning for ages ... Now George has got a problem. His granddaughter.'

Thérèse, who was setting the table for lunch, stopped what she was doing and looked at Charles anxiously.

'What kind of problem? You mean the granddaughter who lives in London and never calls?'

'That's the one. Except that now, she does call. Françoise must have asked her to. Well, I don't know what goes on between those two but the point is, Adèle called and now George is panicking.'

Thérèse was staring down at the tablecloth. Charles went on.

'Now George isn't the kind to let people walk all over him. But when it comes to his daughter, it's another story. He says she'll have him put in a home if she finds out what he's planning.'

Annie, with her baby on her knee, asked her grandfather:

'Do you really think Françoise would do that?'

'Well, I dunno ... she isn't exactly easy-going.'

'I guess she gets that from her dad!' interrupted Franck, who still had memories of one particular stormy encounter with George.

'Oh for heavens' sake!' Thérèse exclaimed loudly. '*Stop* getting so het up about Françoise. She said she wasn't going to call for two months, so this is your chance! Go and do your Tour the way you planned and everything will be fine.'

'Yes, but … I suppose I just find this … this radio silence a bit weird. She didn't say anything to you?'

'No, no. Well, I mean … No more than she did to you, I don't suppose,' answered Thérèse, avoiding his gaze.

Annie tried to distract Justine, who was reaching for the knives on the table. To keep her happy she gave the baby her mobile phone, which Justine immediately tried to put in her mouth.

'And if she did turn up out of the blue, she'd call me straight away and I'd take care of it, and of her. So stop obsessing about the daughter, and the granddaughter for that matter, and off you go!' said Thérèse.

'Still,' said Charles, 'we've got to do something about Adèle, otherwise George will never agree to it. Right everyone, lunchtime.'

Suddenly, the phone that Justine had in her little plump hands started to make unexpected sounds. Annie managed to wrangle it back from her and looked at the screen.

'What's she done to it? Oh no, what does that mean, "Call divert activated"? She's gone and changed all the settings, it's stopped working. Franck! Justine's mucked around with the phone and now it's saying "call divert" or something …'

Wearily, Franck took the phone and, wiping the dribble from the screen with his sleeve, pressed a few buttons and put the phone into his jeans pocket.

Charles looked at Franck, and then down at his plate, and then at Franck again. Finally, he asked:

'So what does that "call divert" thing do?'

'Well, if I choose to divert calls to your home phone, when

people call me on my mobile, the calls will go straight to your landline.'

'But they don't know that's happening?'

'They don't know.'

'And you can do that with landlines as well?'

'Yes, you should be able to.'

'Well, I'll be damned.'

He got up from the table noisily. Thérèse sighed.

'Charles, my veal is going to go cold.'

'Thérèse, what did you do with the phone directory?'

Charles was hopping with excitement. Half an hour and a conversation with Franck later, he went over to George's place.

Justine smiled, showing her two teeth.

George was woken from his slumber by the sound of Charles's footsteps in the garage, but they sounded different from normal. Had he really been asleep for that long? The clock next to the fridge was showing 1.30 p.m.

Charles burst into the room and shouted confidently:

'George, there's no need to worry. There's a solution to the Adèle problem.'

'But isn't it—?' George began.

'What's your mobile number?'

George had to lever himself painfully out of his garden seat and walk out into the corridor to the telephone table. 'There it is,' he said to Charles, pointing at the notecard tacked to the wall next to the postcards of London, on which Françoise had written in her beautiful handwriting: 'Your mobile number: 06 20 15 89 15.'

Charles pulled a piece of paper covered in code out of his

pocket, picked up the landline phone, and after very carefully keying in several different combinations of numbers, hashes and stars, he replaced the handset with an almost solemn expression on his face.

'Right,' said Charles, who seemed to be waiting for something.

'Right,' said George, who was wondering if Charles was going to give him an explanation or whether he was going to have to get it out of him himself. 'Right, well, so that's …'

'Where's your mobile?'

'I think it's in the chest of drawers in the living room, under the card set.'

'OK, here's what you have to do,' said Charles, who now seemed to know what he was doing. 'You're going to go and get it. I'm going to go back home and then I'm going to call you and we'll see which of the two phones ring.'

'But what number are you going to ring me on?'

'The landline number.'

'So it's the home phone that's going to ring, then.'

'No, actually,' answered Charles. 'If it's worked, the mobile should ring.'

George looked at him with a slightly pitying expression.

'I see,' he replied gently, deciding that it was better to say nothing than to worry everyone now. Still, it was a shame that Charles was losing his marbles. And at such a young age.

Charles left, feeling gratified that his friend's knowledge of telecommunications made his own seem fairly extensive. He was back in less than five minutes, only to find George sitting in his chair again.

'And? Which one rang?'

'Oh, neither of them.'

Charles looked perplexed. 'You weren't asleep, were you?'

'Not a bit of it! I was wide awake and there was no ringing. But which number did you ring?'

'05 49 57 68 34.'

'Well, there you go,' said George. 'That's the landline. What was all that stuff you were doing on it? Now it's not working. Thanks a lot!'

'But I don't understand,' said Charles, sounding annoyed. 'It's the mobile that should have rung. Now I'll have to get back on the phone to France Telecom …'

'But Charles,' said George kindly, 'of course the mobile didn't ring, you called the landline. And anyway, the mobile wouldn't ring even if you did call it: it's switched off.'

'It's switched off! Well that explains it! Where is it?'

George handed him a brand-new phone inside a spotless plastic cover. It had clearly never been used.

'I'm going to take it with me. I'll be back in a bit,' said Charles, who was already halfway to the garage.

George sat back down in his chair, reflecting that it was the fate of all elderly people to lose the plot eventually, and he tried to go back to sleep in order to banish this depressing thought. He was going to have to break it to Charles that they weren't going. But before he could think of how to do it, Charles was back. His hip must have been in a frightfully good mood that day.

'It works, dammit, it works! I'll explain it to you.'

Adèle could call him at home all she liked; she'd never know a thing! They were free to do the Tour in peace. Charles initiated George into the mysteries of call diversion, and while he was about it, the wonderful world of modern communication in general – in such depth and detail that his veal and carrots were put in the fridge in a Tupperware container, along with his salad and his rice pudding. He even missed his Ricoré coffee and his four o'clock hot chocolate … His boyish enthusiasm had triumphed over his stomach and most importantly, it had silenced George's voices. They had gone quiet out of politeness. Because voices can torment a man, drive him mad with doubt and sing the praises of laziness and cowardice. But they know not to get in the way of neighbours.

Six days later, a metallic blue Renault Scenic with satnav and sunroof was approaching the bend in the tree-lined road in Chanteloup, sparkling in the proud late September sun. In the rear-view mirror, George watched Charles's family waving them off. He saw Thérèse wipe away a tear as the house where he had lived for eighty-three years became smaller and smaller, until it had disappeared entirely behind the trees. His chest felt heavy and there was a lump in his throat, but he had no regrets. As for Charles, he was driving with one hand and waving the other out of the window, and looked utterly ecstatic. With one hundred and fifty-nine years between them, they set off on the Tour de France.

Thursday 25 September

Chanteloup (Deux-Sèvres)–Notre-Dame-de-Monts (Vendée)

Their epic journey in the Renault Scenic was to follow the itinerary of the 2008 Tour de France to the letter. This was made up of twenty-one stages (except that George and Charles's Tour would leave out stage 4, as they had decided not to count the individual time trial in Cholet). They had given themselves two or three days to complete each stage, so that they could explore the surrounding area a little. But they were to change hotel almost every night. Their route was planned out as follows:

Stage 1: Brest–Plumelec
Stage 2: Auray–Saint-Brieuc
Stage 3: Saint-Malo–Nantes
Stage 5: Cholet–Châteauroux
Stage 6: Aigurande–Super-Besse

Stage 7: Brioude–Aurillac
Stage 8: Figeac–Toulouse
Stage 9: Toulouse–Bagnères-de-Bigorre
Stage 10: Pau–Hautacam
Stage 11: Lannemezan–Foix
Stage 12: Lavelanet–Narbonne
Stage 13: Narbonne–Nîmes
Stage 14: Nîmes–Digne-les-Bains
Stage 15: Embrun–Prato Nevoso
Stage 16: Cuneo–Jausiers
Stage 17: Embrun–L'Alpe-d'Huez
Stage 18: Le Bourg-d'Oisans–Saint-Étienne
Stage 19: Roanne–Montluçon
Stage 20: Cérilly–Saint-Amand-Montrond
Stage 21: Étampes–Paris Champs-Élysées

Three extra stages had been added to take them from Chanteloup to the official starting point at Brest – which, as Charles pointed out, was 'a heck of a way away'. He had called them stage 0 (Chanteloup–Notre-Dame-de-Monts, staying with Charles's sister, Ginette Bruneau), stage 0a (Notre-Dame-de-Monts–Gâvres, overnighting with Charles's cousin Odette Fonteneau), and finally stage 0b (Gâvres–Brest).

They started by taking the first turn out of Chanteloup. As they went, the little roads with dandelions growing in the cracks were replaced by roads whose surface had been fixed so often it resembled a tarmac patchwork. They passed many familiar names on the rusty signposts: La Timarière, La Châtaigneraie,

Le Bout du Monde. Then white strips started to appear on the road and all of a sudden they were driving alongside lorries and trucks. That's when they knew they were really on their way.

The car was not full: the only things in the boot were George's little suitcase and Charles's large one – twice as big as his companion's, in fact, and much more modern, with wheels (when Charles went travelling, he did so in style) – as well as a whole box of tourist guides. The one for Southern Brittany had been put in the glove compartment, along with the GPS user manual and Charles's Vichy pastilles. Thérèse had also provided them with a picnic set – they couldn't go eating in restaurants every day, after all. She had even managed to sneak in a little crate of tomatoes from the garden and some ham won in a round of *belote* without them noticing.

George and Charles did not talk much in the car, which still smelled of new leather. Apart from the silky and monotonous tones of the GPS, it was a rather silent journey. There was an atmosphere of reflection, and contemplation. Autumn had barely arrived, the leaves were just starting to change colour, but it was still a beautiful sight. George, who had not left his small corner of the world for years, sat back and took it in.

On the route from Deux-Sèvres to the Vendée they passed through sleepy villages with geraniums in the windows, smart houses covered in Virginia creeper, and church steeples breaking through the clouds. Bit by bit, the landscape changed as they drove on. The green palette was flecked with a hint of yellow here, a touch of black there. The undulating forests flattened out into windswept plains. Now and then a windmill would come into view, or a thatched cottage hidden amongst the pine trees, or a sign towards a campsite or the salt flats. They were approaching the sea.

Notre-Dame-de-Monts was a clean, discreet seaside town. What was particularly charming about it was the lack of high-rise buildings. This part of the Vendée had suffered from a wave of construction in the 1970s that had left a number of towns in the area permanently scarred. The beautiful beach ten kilometres down the coast in Saint-Jean-de-Monts had been blighted by concrete monstrosities, fast-food chains and noisy arcades. Notre-Dame-de-Monts, on the other hand, had been miraculously spared, its houses set well back from the lovely seafront, screened by the long grass on the dunes. All of this was familiar to Charles, as he had often come to visit his sister, who lived here all year round. But this was George's first time in the town, and he was enchanted by what he saw.

They arrived at 11.30 a.m. As they were not expected at their hostess's until lunchtime and didn't wish to impose, the travelling companions decided to go and admire the sea, which sparkled beyond the flags lining the esplanade. The sun, which had barely made an appearance all summer, was warming the sand on the beach and encouraging the last of the summer holidaymakers to linger. With their feet in the sand and their eyes gazing out over the Atlantic, George and Charles were happy, even if they didn't yet dare express it to each other.

It was almost as if the two neighbours had become shy of one another. The fact was their friendship had played out against the same background for thirty years (almost forty, come to think of it). They shared cups of tea in front of the weather report. They celebrated birthdays and family events together. Initially they had been the kinds of neighbours who invited each other for the dessert and coffee courses until one day, about fifteen years ago, Charles had invited George and his wife – perhaps by accident, perhaps not – for the starter and main course as well, when the conversation was still serious, ties were still in place and sisters-in-law were still being polite. Their friendship had also sustained a lively trade in lettuces, screwdrivers, pokers, freezer bags, various types of string, cousins' addresses and small favours. The same routine had suited them both for all this time; God knows why they had decided to play adventurers and give it all up now!

All of a sudden, there on the seafront at Notre-Dame-de-Monts, they no longer knew what to say to each other. Their friendship was breathing in new air; time would tell if it would survive the change.

George and Charles arrived at Ginette's house at twelve-thirty on the dot. Kisses, did you have a good trip, well, a bit of traffic around Le Perrier as always, but otherwise yes, it was fine, the weather's still nice, you've brought the sun with you, it was such bad weather this summer, yes fine, can't complain. It was the same exchange they had every year, a game of question and answer that they knew off by heart, where everyone spoke at the same time as if joining in with the chorus of a song they knew and loved.

Ginette suggested eating on the patio, where the table was already set. Was it the Atlantic air or perhaps the sweet scent of the pine trees he could smell as they drank their coffee in the garden? George hadn't felt this good in years. He had met Ginette a few times at family lunches, and he had always found her a little haughty. But seeing her in her own home she seemed very different. She scarcely looked seventy-three with her reddish hair, cropped trousers and orange plastic sandals. He had never before noticed her youthful energy – or perhaps widowhood suited her? Whatever it was, here in her own garden Ginette's manner was much more playful and her natural authoritativeness was at once heightened and yet more agreeable, like the autumn wind that rustled the stone pines. And perhaps a little like this dangerously drinkable plum brandy.

Charles was keeping an eye on him. For George, having fallen for the charms of Ginette, or of her plum brandy, or perhaps both at once, was beginning to make a fool of himself. He suddenly remembered lyrics to songs he had not sung for sixty years. He recounted the numerous glories of the Tour that they were going to relive one by one, stories of the past told in the future tense. The shy neighbours had found their tongues again.

They moved from brandy to chocolate, from Petit Chinon to herbal tea. The afternoon turned to evening and the evening became night. After a dinner that was no less sumptuous than their lunch, it was time for a round of rummy.

Ginette got out her playing mat and the two decks of cards. George was already sitting at the table in the living room, hunched over his tea. It even looked as though he might already be sleeping off the plum brandy. As she dealt the cards, Ginette asked:

'And George, your granddaughter, Adèle, how is she getting on over there, in London? She works in film, doesn't she?'

'Yes, but I don't know what she actually does. Well, I suppose it was her decision … She never tells me anything, you see.'

George suddenly felt very low – no doubt a side effect of the drink – and Ginette was in turn overcome by a wave of melancholy.

'That's how it is with the young nowadays, they always leave …'

'Oh Ginette, young people have always left home. Even we did.'

'Yes, but we never went far,' Ginette pointed out.

'No, we didn't go far,' Charles interjected. 'But we might as well have done. My parents were still in Bressuire when I left to move in with Thérèse in '54. Before Chanteloup we were down in Pougne-Hérisson, near Parthenay. Now, travelling twenty-five kilometres to see the family doesn't take long these days, but you've got to remember that in '54, twenty-five kilometres on a bike was a real slog – it felt much further than it does today! It's not like we were there every weekend, and we didn't spend hours on the phone, or on the internet, or emailing each other or I don't know what else. With young people today, the further away they are, the more they're on your back all the time. Don't get me wrong, I'm not complaining. But sometimes … George, it's your turn.'

George looked distractedly at his hand, before continuing in the same vein.

'Yes, yes, the telephone. Argh! They're all *glued* to their telephones, like you wouldn't believe! It was bad enough before, even if a phone came in handy now and again. But now with all these mobile phones—'

'And it gets worse,' Charles cut in. 'Wait 'til you hear this.

My grandson from Parthenay, right, he comes to stay with us in the holidays. And he's only reading his emails, that's right, his *internet emails* on his mobile phone!' To underline the absurdity of the thing he banged his fist on the table emphatically and leaned back in his chair. 'I mean, I've seen that kind of thing on telly, but I just thought no, that's for people who are in the know, who work in telecoms, or maybe even a couple of the big CEOs, but no! My grandson! A butcher in Parthenay!'

George shook his head. 'If even butchers need computers all over the place, what is the world coming to! Right, where were we? Wait, Ginette, what are you doing?'

'Going out,' announced Ginette proudly.

'Already?' exclaimed Charles. 'With all of your cards?'

'Yep, and without a joker!'

'My, my … And there I was with nothing. Have a look at that hand, not even a face card, totally useless. We take more points without the joker as well, I think …'

'No, no more points, just your admiration, gentlemen … So minus twenty for yours truly and two hundred points each for you two.'

'Well, this is off to a good start … Right, who's dealing?'

'The idiot who asks who's dealing,' guffawed Charles, a regular at the *belote* table.

As George dealt out the cards, Ginette cautiously picked up the conversation.

'But what you say about mobile phones, George … Well, I've got one and—'

George ceased dealing and stopped her there.

'Me too, Ginette, me too, but *I don't use it*!'

'Well, actually you do use it, George,' Charles pointed out. 'You're diverting all of your calls.'

'Yes, but that's different.'

'George is using his phone to make everyone think he's taking it easy in Chanteloup, when actually he's doing the Tour de France,' Charles explained with a wry smile.

'But that's just *so they don't get worried*!'

'And you can do that with mobile phones, can you?' asked Ginette, impressed.

'You certainly can!' Charles answered proudly. 'I'm the one who set it all up, give it a try if you like.'

'Alright Charles,' interrupted George, who had suddenly sobered up. 'Are you playing cards or giving a lecture on technology? It would be great if we could start playing before sunrise.'

'All I'm trying to say,' Ginette began again, 'is that I have a mobile and I think it's great.'

'There you go!' exclaimed George. 'Like I said, women can't get away from their phones.'

'Not at all, and I can prove it: I have a contract that allows me one hour of calls a month. A *month*!'

'Psssh, that's already too much.'

'Well I think it gives you more freedom, in a way. I get out and about a lot more now I have my mobile.'

'Oh right,' laughed Charles, 'because you were living like a nun before?'

'No, I just think mobiles bring people closer.'

'Closer?' said George. 'The reason I live in the country is so

I don't get pestered all the time, so I'm not sure that bringing people closer to me—'

'George,' Charles interrupted, 'you've been living in the country for eighty-three years, it's not like you chose to.'

'No, but if I had been given the choice, I would have chosen to live exactly where I am. So that no one bothers me!'

Nobody had a good hand, and tiredness was starting to set in. The laying of cards had given way to wide yawns. Finally, Ginette was named winner and they put away the mat in the dresser covered in trinkets. It was time to unpack their bags and put on their well-ironed pyjamas.

Ginette's house was large, although she only occupied a small part of it; the rest was rented out in the summer to two families who had come here for their holidays for years. There was no lack of spare rooms, and so George and Charles each had their own.

George brought his things into his new quarters, a small bedroom with a bolster (far better than those little pillow things), a brown chenille bedcover and a large wardrobe that smelled of mothballs. The mattress looked like a good one. And if he was honest, if there was one thing that really scared him about this mad trip, it was the beds they'd have to sleep in. He had brought earplugs for the noise and citronella for the mosquitoes, but bedding was anyone's guess. After carrying out the briefest of ablutions in the small washroom he shared with Charles, he sat on the bed, pulled off his slippers and lay down carefully, breathing a sigh of relief as he did so. This bed would do just fine. He picked up his book, a thriller by Mary Higgins Clark, but found he could not concentrate on it. His head was spinning, buzzing, humming, restless and full of thoughts. It seemed like his mind was trying to tell him something. It had to be said, George was unfortunately prone to occasional rushes of optimism.

Good grief, he was feeling marvellous. It was as though the bed had been made for him, and around him it was as silent as it was in his own home, with nothing but a very quiet rustling if he really listened hard – was it the wind in the pine trees or the sound of the Atlantic? Perhaps he was imagining it. The geometric pattern of the wallpaper in varying shades of beige was soothing, almost hypnotic. The two meals had been delicious, yet unpretentious. George couldn't stand pretentious cooking. Or pretentious anything else, for that matter. The meals had been simple, as if Ginette had not gone to any great pains to prepare them. But fifty years of married life had taught him that she had probably spent the whole morning cooking, and perhaps even the night before as well. Did she cook like that all the time, making simple dishes just how he liked them?

He'd be glad to come here again, as a matter of fact. Would Ginette perhaps invite him back sometime? Maybe they could stay another night instead of stopping off in Gâvres? He didn't really fancy spending a day with cousin Odette. He didn't know her, and didn't feel inclined to change that; she had always sounded rather difficult. And she was a bit of a God-botherer, which was not George's cup of tea at all. What would Charles think of this change of plan? It wouldn't affect the schedule too much, after all, and it would mean they could all go and visit

Noirmoutier together. The island was meant to be spectacular whatever the weather. All these thoughts lulled George into a deep, simple sleep. Perfectly simple.

Friday 26 September

Notre-Dame-de-Monts (Vendée)

The next morning he woke up in a delicious state of confusion. He had slept so well that he woke up with no idea where he was or what time it was. For a few seconds, he felt as good as new. The sun was up. 8.47 a.m. A miracle. He lay in bed without moving a muscle.

Meanwhile, Ginette and Charles were in the kitchen preparing breakfast in their dressing gowns. Ginette was very proud of her kitchen, which was equipped with all the mod cons. Her son had convinced her to have it completely redone two years earlier and she had chosen a red design from Ikea. The trinkets that covered almost every inch of flat surface were the only things that predated the Ikea trip.

They were speaking in low voices because they were talking about George. Ginette had heard he was in a bad way, and asked after his health with the requisite tone of concern. Charles, on the other hand, was not worried.

'Oh, he's fine. George is going to live to be a hundred. He's as strong as an ox, he'll outlive us all.'

'But weren't you telling me that the doctors—'

'No, no, no. Firstly, it's not *the doctors*, it's his GP, who's diagnosed him with all kinds of things over the last twenty years, and is always trying to stuff him with pills. Because George never takes them, his GP is forever convinced he's going to keel over and die any minute. But I'm telling you that's not going to happen any time soon.'

'Glad to hear it.'

'Of course, only I'm not sure he agrees. Everything that's really wrong with George is going on in his head. He's a bit … sort of … depressed. So that's why I thought a change of scene wouldn't do him any harm.'

'A touch of depression then, you think?'

'More than a touch, actually. But don't mention it to him or he'll fly off the handle. Thérèse tried once, she told him about her homeopath in Bressuire. Apparently homeopathy is quite good for stuff like that. Well, he told her where to go, and that was the end of that.'

'Shhhh!' said Ginette, hearing George's footsteps in the corridor.

'He'll live to be a hundred, I'm telling you,' Charles murmured emphatically.

'Morning everyone!' George boomed. He looked as fresh as a daisy. 'I slept marvellously. Hats off to your bed, Ginette.'

'That's good to hear! Coffee, George?'

'Why not!'

Breakfast was a masterclass in theatrical asides, with Ginette muttering to her brother, 'He seems on top form, for someone who's got depression'; George whispering to Charles about his proposed change of itinerary; Charles privately asking Ginette if they could impose for another night; and George anxiously nagging Charles for the answer.

Finally, when the bread had been put away and the bowls had been washed and dried, they were all agreed that Charles and George would stay another night, a plan that suited everyone. The two companions would leave early the next morning, have lunch in Gâvres with the cousin, and then off they would go to Brest, the first step of the 2008 Tour, where they had booked a room at the Hôtel du Centre. In the meantime, they would go cockle picking in the Passage du Gois in Noirmoutier, the very spot where Olano had waved a dramatic farewell to his chances of winning the Tour in '99. His head full of optimism, and anecdotes from Tours gone by, George began a day that would hold a special place in his pacemaker-fitted heart.

Saturday 27 September

Brest (Finistère)

Adèle looked at her watch. 8.57 p.m. France was an hour ahead, so it was a bit late to call her grandfather. She had promised herself she would call him once a week; that was ten days ago. She had kept missing her moment. But she remembered the Saturday-night entertainment show must still be going, so there was a chance he would answer. Her grandfather picked up at the second ring.

'Hello, Adèle?' he said, sounding much more cheerful than usual.

'Yes, Grandpa, it's me,' she replied, a little surprised. 'How are you, Grandpa?'

'Fine, great, I'm just sitting in the living room, watching the telly.'

Something wasn't quite right. Admittedly, Adèle's phone calls were rare, but normally she could have predicted in advance exactly what her grandfather would say. The only time it had been different had been when her grandmother had died. Her grandfather didn't sound natural, and the TV was turned right up. She heard a strange voice in the background: 'At the roundabout, take the second exit.'

She double-checked that it was the landline she had called.

'Are you sure everything's alright, Grandpa?'

He took a few moments to reply, and she heard a murmuring sound, almost a hissing.

'Yes, everything's fine, nothing to report really. Everything fine with you?'

'Yes, everything—'

'Great, well, lots of love!'

'Grandpa, have you got people round?'

'No, there's no one else here, I'm just watching tele—'

BAM! A deafening sound like a gunshot rang down the line.

'Grandpa, what's going on? GRANDPA!'

The line went dead before Adèle could work out what was happening. She redialled the number frantically. The phone rang and rang, but no answer. She tried the mobile. Same thing. Her heart was racing, and her imagination went into overdrive. Had it really been a gunshot? An explosion? Maybe his stove ... That stove was as old as Methuselah. It must have blown up. Or a thief with a gun? Most farmers had a shotgun out there in the sticks. What could she do? Call the police? But what was the number of the French police? At last her grandfather picked up.

'Grandpa? Grandpa, are you alright? Are you hurt?'

'Oh sweetheart,' George replied shakily.

'What's going on?' Adèle asked with panic in her voice.

'Promise me you won't tell your mother.'

Adèle was taken aback but somewhat reassured. If he was hatching secret plans to fool his daughter, things could not be as bad as all that.

'But Grandpa, what—'

'Adèle, sweetheart,' answered her grandfather, sounding a little more stable now. 'Nothing's wrong, but you have to promise me not to say anything to your mother, otherwise she'll get hysterical and that won't be good for any of us.'

Adèle reluctantly agreed. And so her grandfather explained that they were in the car, and that Charles had tried to turn off the sound of 'the nice lady in the GPS', but that he had got the wrong button, and while he was hurriedly trying all the knobs and buttons in the Scenic, he hadn't seen the car in front slowing down to turn right.

'But how come you're in a car when I'm calling your landline? And where are you anyway?'

'We're about thirty kilometres from Brest. We've diverted the calls.'

'From Brest? In *Brittany*?'

'Yes, in Finistère.'

Her grandfather's house in Chanteloup. Brest. The two places were at least five hundred kilometres apart.

'But, Grandpa, what on earth are you doing in Brest?'

'We've decided to do the Tour de France.'

'Grandpa, don't tell me—'

'No, no, not on bikes. We're only doing it in a car.'

Just to clarify, Adèle replied, 'Three thousand kilometres in a car.'

Her grandfather felt a rush of pride. It was the first time that someone had found it impressive. He couldn't help adding:

'Three thousand five hundred, actually.'

But he instantly regretted saying it.

'And the doctors, have you seen your doctor, what did he say about it?'

'Pffff ... you know what doctors are like. Damned idiots, the lot of them.'

'You're not on your own, though, are you? Have you at least told someone what you're doing?'

'Charles is with me, and his whole family knows, they even encouraged us to do it,' said George, cackling ruefully to himself.

'OK. But Grandpa, why the Tour de France?'

'Because that's what we wanted to do.'

This straightforward answer took her by surprise. It was an endearing response, touching even, and made her grandfather seem more human, ageless, a bit like herself, a bit like everyone else. It was normal to want to go away, just like that.

'So are we agreed? Not a word to your mother.'

And suddenly everything came back to her: the pills, his fading eyesight, his rheumatism, and all the clichés that accompany old age. Finally she said, with a hint of irritation:

'I don't know, Grandpa, you know what Mum's like ... And you are taking risks with your health.'

'Adèle, I'm not dead yet, you know.'

'Right, well, I've got to go, Grandpa. I'll ... I'll call you later.'

*

It was almost midnight. George and Charles had finally arrived at the Hôtel du Centre in Brest, three hours later than they had intended. They had been badly shaken by the accident. It was not the first time either of them had been in a crash, but this one had been so unexpected, so ridiculous and surreal that they were both still in shock. It was almost enough to make them regret ever having started the Tour. It looked as though the first step could end up being the last. And yet. And yet the adventure had got off to such a good start ... especially for George.

George and Ginette had got along famously. Even Charles, who was not the most perceptive person at the best of times, had picked up on it. They had hung around for so long in Notre-Dame-de-Monts that they had simply struck the stopover in Gâvres from their itinerary – and Charles's cousin with it. Charles had initially been reluctant to call her with a trumped-up excuse, but had ended up grudgingly complying, rolling his eyes like a moody teenager. The three friends had enjoyed another exquisite meal on Ginette's patio. Over coffee, as George and Charles were starting to think about getting going, Ginette, who, like most women, never missed a trick, announced that she would be joining them in Nantes. Just to 'say hello'. Apparently it would also be a good chance to visit a few friends in the area, and for her to treat herself to a bit of window-shopping. Not that she intended to buy anything, of course, because of the credit crunch.

Charles and George were aiming to get to Nantes on Tuesday 7 October. George could picture it already: the two heroes of the Tour arriving to an adoring crowd, which was made up principally of Ginette. Charles replied in a mock-severe tone that the athletes' wives were strictly forbidden from all parts of the Tour. But George, on cracking form, found a quick comeback. 'Ah, but that's perfect,' he said, 'seeing as Ginette is neither your wife nor mine, and the rules clearly state that the Tour is open to "any and all wild-card entries".' Ginette feigned a blush and Charles said, chuckling, 'Well, if it's in the rules …'

They drank to the rules with a small glass of plum brandy (only one finger for Charles, who was driving). In order not to miss each other in Nantes, Ginette showed her brother and George how to save her number in George's phone. She wrote 'Ginette Bruneau', along with her home and mobile numbers, and took George's details too. They promised to call each other to arrange a time and a place to meet. These happy moments changed George's idea of what the Tour was going to be like, but there was one thing he had never been more sure of: nobody would be putting him in a home any time soon.

Now, sitting alone in his yellow and grey room in the Hôtel du Centre, looking at the old suitcase that he had not yet unpacked, he reflected with deep sadness that nothing was less certain.

He had imagined he would get away with it without anyone trying to stop him, and now the whole plan was out in the open. For three days he had been feeling more like himself, his old self, only to become once again the doddering grandpa with all his aches and pains, who was not to do anything in case he got too tired, and did himself harm. It was his own fault: he had so often indulged in the comfort of other people's sympathy. It had never made the pain go away, but it had made him feel less hopeless. Now what he really needed was freedom, and, surprise, surprise, he found that he was refused it. George thought of Adèle. Would she tell her mother? Of course she would, that was why she had called him on that first evening. To keep an eye on him. And of course, she had caught him with his hand in the cookie jar. He would have liked to talk all this over with Charles, but he couldn't face getting up. He felt chained to his bed, in this yellow and grey bedroom.

The sound of the phone ringing made him jump.

'Grandpa?'

'Yes?'

'OK, good, you've got your phone on you.'

'Yes, yes,' said George wearily.

'Do you know how to write texts?'

'Erm ...'

'You know, the messages people send with mobile phones.'

'Oh yes, I know what you mean, but sending them ... well, that's another story ...'

'OK, ask Charles, or at the hotel reception, they'll show you how.'

'But why do you want me to write texts?'

'Because you're going to send me one every day,' said Adèle firmly, a hint of mischief in her voice.

George was beginning to feel hopeful. She hadn't said anything about Françoise.

'Every evening, Grandpa, you're going to send me a text. One, to let me know *how* you are, and two, to let me know *where* you are.'

'How I am and where I am. Got it.'

'Every evening, OK? If a night goes by without one, I'm coming to find you and I'm telling Mum. OK?'

'OK, it's a deal. No need to worry, I'll send you one every evening. Right. Even this evening?'

'Yes, even this evening, as a test run. You can send them whenever, I work nights.'

'OK, fine. Was there ... anything else?'

'No, but take care of yourself, Grandpa, OK?'

'Will do, sweetheart. OK, bye now.'

He hung up before Adèle had the chance to answer, and hurried over to Charles's room.

'Charles, my friend, the Tour needs you!'

Adèle stood alone in the middle of the cluttered, dimly lit set, trying to get to grips with what she had just found out. That he'd diverted his calls. His rather feeble attempt to pull the wool over her eyes. That he'd been in an accident. And now the Tour de France. When all this time she had imagined him comfortably ensconced in his armchair! Was his heart going to be able to cope with all this? Ought she just to have told him to go back home and contacted her mother? Françoise had been quite clear: she didn't wish to be troubled for the next two months except in a real emergency. Did her grandfather gallivanting up and down the roads of France count as a real emergency? No, probably not. Adèle had memories of him obsessively following the Tour de France on television. She had been little at the time, but she remembered the men talking loudly around the TV set. Yes, he was old and ill, but he was still responsible for his own actions.

He wasn't a child. And yet she had just treated him like one, a child who has to call his parents every five minutes to reassure them everything is fine. It was complicated, and Adèle regretted getting involved in the first place. She of all people, who had taken so little notice of her grandparents for so long …

The familiar sounds of the film set brought her back to reality – if you could call it that. This crooked house, which was the setting, the stage and the main character of the film, had been her whole life for the last eleven days. The actors were sitting on the black wooden steps in their post-war costumes, devouring their dinner from plastic plates and chatting with the technicians, who were dressed in jeans. It was time Adèle made her own visit to the canteen, which had been set up on the ground floor.

She felt less stressed than she had during the first few days, but also much less enthused. She was beginning to get to know the team not only in professional terms (who did what, who answered to whom), but also on a personal level, and those she connected with were few and far between. She did her best to avoid everyone else. It wasn't that Adèle was antisocial; in fact she had a lot of friends. Two hundred and nineteen on Facebook at last count. But, to use her grandfather's expression, sometimes she just wanted to be left the hell alone, especially in a job she wasn't being paid to do. So she kept her distance, even from those whose company she found perfectly pleasant. In a place where excessive familiarity was the norm, she stuck to polite and strictly professional exchanges. She had spent enough time on film sets to know that friendships formed there were as fake as the actors' moustaches. People became friends for life after three takes, and forgot each other before the wrap party hangover had lifted. It was better not to make friends at all, in order to avoid disappointment.

When she had filled her plate with whatever unappetising dish was on offer that day, she went back up the three flights of stairs to have her meal in peace in the production office. Unfortunately, there were two other girls already eating there and she couldn't refuse their invitation to join them. Michelle and Sophie, second production assistant and assistant make-up artist respectively, were very similar: they were both almost thirty, pretty in a bland sort of a way, obviously came from privileged backgrounds, spoke very quickly, and tried hard to hide their posh accents. It was nothing like the conversations she once imagined took place on film sets: on shoots where everyone was paid fairly for the work they did, where people's individual talents were allowed to shine, people would talk about the influence of the Nouvelle Vague, the films of Wong Kar-wai or the remastered versions of Cassavetes' classics, all in between two perfect takes. In reality, Michelle and Sophie were talking about Steve, the sound engineer, who had cheated on his wife with Sally, the continuity girl, in the toilets of the Swan pub, and about the big booze-up on Tuesday night, which apparently had been even bigger than the one on Monday night.

At times like this, Adèle seriously considered packing it all in. Her job was ridiculous. She fetched the actors' coffees and anything else they required, made the extras wait around when shooting was delayed by five hours, recharged the walkie-talkies, and roamed the streets to find the owner of the car whose alarm was holding up shooting. She worked fifteen hours a day, six days a week, for no pay. It would have been different if she were learning something! But she wasn't learning anything, apart from knowledge of the sexual exploits of Sally the continuity girl. Most of the time she was nowhere near the set, or there was no space in the room where a scene was being shot, especially not for a runner. She never got to see any of the things she was interested in and dreamed of one day making a Hollywood career out of: the cinematography, directing the actors – in essence, the creative process.

And on top of that, she had to put up with the most vulgar conversations. If only Irving Ferns was still here! He had been on set for the first two days of filming, playing the role of the grandfather killed at the beginning of the story. She had spent more time with the eighty-one-year-old actor than with anyone in the crew, and she had enjoyed his company a good deal more than that of any of the empty-headed assistants. He would be back towards the end of the schedule to shoot a couple of flashback scenes. But would he remember her? Friendships were short-lived here, and he had seemed in a strange mood when he left.

She was distracted from these gloomy thoughts by the sound of her phone – she had got a text. She couldn't help smiling as she read it:

Grandpa 27/09/2008 23:35
Hotl du Cntr, Brest. All gd.
(Hôtel du Centre, Brest. All good.)

And then almost immediately after:

Grandpa, 27/09/2008 23:36
Hotl du Cntr, Brest, Fnstr. All gd.
(Hôtel du Centre, Brest, Finistère. All good.)

It was a good excuse to slip out of the cramped office. She raced down the stairs, went out into the street, threw her plate of barely touched food into the nearest bin and texted back:

OK

She stood out in the cool evening air for a little while, but no reply came. Having been rattled by her grandfather's accident and a growing sense of disillusionment, she realised that this exchange had lifted her spirits. Where had her grandfather learned text language? He had never sent a text message in his life. It was funny to think of her grandfather, who rarely ventured beyond his vegetable patch, starting to write like that! Come to think of it, it was quite brave, what he was doing. Mad, bonkers even, but brave. 'Because that's what we wanted to do.' She smiled again. At that age ... You had to admire him.

He must have spent months planning the expedition; must have gone over the route a thousand times in his head. He must have had moments of doubt, told himself it was too ambitious. She hoped it would live up to his expectations. And she understood better than most about dreams that end in disappointment.

Well, that's one thing off my list! George thought to himself. The text had been sent, the text had been received, and so his granddaughter would leave him alone for the moment. But the bizarre spelling that was clearly required to write the things was totally perplexing. Adèle hadn't warned him about this. It was going to be a problem: he was certain that it would not always be as easy to find someone to write his texts for him as it had been here.

The story of how these texts came to be sent went like this: Charles had not been any help at all, so George had had to go and ask at reception, which was very quiet at that time of night. He had to interrupt the receptionist, most likely an intern of no more than twenty who was deep in discussion with another girl, probably a friend who had come to keep her company. He explained the problem. The two girls seemed to find the request rather amusing and asked excitedly what they were supposed to write.

'Hôtel du Centre, comma, Brest, full stop. All good, full stop.'

The girls got him to enter Adèle's number into his phone and then showed him how to type a message and send it. And with three clicks the message was on its way – to London! He then asked them to send it again because he had forgotten to write 'Finistère' after 'Brest'. It was a chance to go over everything he had just learned. But he was not convinced. What he saw on the screen resembled only vaguely what he was trying to say: 'Hôtel du Centre, comma, Brest, comma, Finistère, full stop.' Most of the vowels were missing; the word 'Finistère' didn't have any vowels at all. George was almost ashamed to send it to Adèle: he was very strict about spelling and had told his granddaughter countless times when she was little that flawless spelling was the key to success. She had always made him proud by coming first in class dictations.

He plucked up the courage to point out:

'But young lady ... I mean ... the spelling is a little ...'

'Yes, but you see texts have their own spelling. Text language is a bit odd, but it's cool, you'll see.'

'Ah, OK, it's got its own spelling has it? But why can't you just write normally?'

The young girl thought for a moment, and it was her friend who finally answered him:

'It works better if you write them in text language. It's, like, quicker.'

George nodded as if he understood. He would have liked to learn more but three English tourists had just arrived with all their suitcases and it was time for him to go up to his room.

On his way back upstairs, he received a reply from Adèle. 'OK.' This text language was rather annoying but it had helped take his mind off other things. Adèle's little message had made him happy. He looked at it several times, but then it was gone, lost in his phone, and he couldn't get it back. At least he knew it was in there somewhere. It was like getting a little postcard. That would really make the girls downstairs laugh, an old fogey saying that text messages were like postcards. But still, it had made him happy.

Sunday 28 September

Brest (Finistère)

George and Charles spent the day exploring the town. George remembered photographs of Brest's proud arsenal as it stood before the war, with its castle and beautiful ships. But as he kept saying to Charles, the Germans had blown everything up. Wide, dead-straight roads, concrete high-rises and depressing architecture had risen from the rubble. On the receptionist's advice, the two friends headed for the harbour, which was more authentic and had more going on than the centre of town.

By the time they arrived, they had worked up a thirst, but all the café terraces were overrun with teenagers with funny haircuts. In search of a café 'like the ones back home', they walked along the docks amid cranes and green and red buoys, disused railway lines and rusted grain carts, and soon forgot what it was they had set out to look for. It was a nice day and the sea air was refreshing, even if it did smell slightly of petrol. Their stroll took them right up to the marina at the far end of the harbour. Down a side street, they happened upon Chez Odile, where they settled down to a steak and chips, followed by cheese and coffee. They made slow progress back to the car: they needed time to digest. George managed to take a nap during the ten-minute drive back to the hotel, where they had a well-earned siesta.

It was 6.30 p.m., and Charles had been banging on about one thing all day: he had come to Brittany to eat *galettes bretonnes.* The hotel reception recommended Crêperie Saint-Malo, just around the corner. At quarter to seven, they were the first diners in the restaurant. Charles was in a great mood, but his travelling companion was squirming in his seat. Eventually, when he couldn't keep quiet any longer, George took the bull by the horns.

'So, just to be clear, you have no idea how to write texts?'

'Not a clue.'

'Right, because … I have to send one to Adèle this evening. Which is a nice idea, but I don't know how to write them.'

'What do you mean, you don't know how? You sent one last night, didn't you?'

'Well, as far as the technology goes, I've got it. It's not actually that complicated, you know. But anyway, the point is, there's a special language. You can't just write a text like you'd write … I dunno, a postcard. You see, it doesn't pack the same punch if it's written normally,' said George sagely, as if this were a universally acknowledged truth.

'No, no, of course not,' agreed Charles, not wanting to seem out of touch.

'But I'm no expert when it comes to text language.'

'So how did Adèle write her text, then?'

'Well, she didn't exactly reply in detail ... It's hard to tell from just one word.'

'Of course.'

Charles wasn't sure what to make of this. Everyone wrote text messages. Even his friends in the senior citizens' club did it. They were no sharper than him – quite the opposite in fact – and he found it hard to believe you had to go to the lengths of learning a foreign language (well not strictly foreign, but as good as) just to send a little text message. Then again, if it was true, he was the one who was going to look stupid and all things considered, it was better not to seem daft.'You should have told me earlier,' said Charles. 'I would have asked my grandson Jonathan, in Niort. He'd know for sure, he spends his whole day sending text messages.'

'You couldn't give him a ring, could you?'

'I don't think it can really be explained over the phone ... I'm sure we can find someone here to show us the ropes.'

The two men ordered some cider. Wearily, George went on.

'It could even be that there aren't any rules. You know how they just make up words these days, and even worse, they do it in *Franglais*, you know,' he said, throwing up his hands in despair.

'It's not that slang *verlan*, is it? At least with *verlan* there are proper rules, and it's not even that complicated. You just switch the syllables around.'

'There are rules alright, but it's not exactly poetry, is it?' sighed George.

Charles did likewise for form. Truth be told, he didn't have much of an opinion on the matter.

'That's an interesting point, though,' said George. 'Take pig Latin, for example – or *louchébem*, as we butchers called it. That had rules. And say what you like, it had a kind of poetry as well. I'm not saying it was great art or anything ... but at least it had a bit of style, a bit of panache. And it was a good laugh. Sorry, but *verlan* isn't half as much fun.'

'Ah yes, they called it the "butchers' slang" ... My uncle could speak it, but I never really got the hang of it.'

'Well of course, you weren't a butcher.'

'Neither was my uncle. He was a greengrocer.'

'The thing about pig Latin was that it was democratic, anyone could speak it, all you had to do was learn the rules and it was a piece of cake.'

'I don't remember it being as simple as all that.'

'Oh come on, Charles!' said George indignantly. 'It was perfectly simple. Right. Take *igpay*. As you know, that means pig. All you do is move the *p* to the end of the word, and tack on the syllable "ay". And there you go.'

'OK, I see,' said Charles. 'When you put it like that, it sounds easy. So, for example, egg would be ... *ggeay*.'

'Actually, no, because it's too difficult to pronounce. For words starting with vowels, you just add "way" to the end. And that's where the real poetry comes in. You have to judge it by the sound of the word.'

'Judge it by the sound of the word.'

'Exactly. It has to flow. So I would say ... *eggway*!'

'*Eggway*,' repeated Charles, looking thoughtful. 'You're right, you can't say it isn't poetic. But I still don't think it's "a piece of cake".'

'But it is! Of course, you have to get used to it, but anyone can speak pig Latin.'

George saw the head waiter approaching their table and looked at Charles with a mischievous glint in his eye.

'OK, now you can speak pig Latin. Yes you can, don't be shy, you can do it. So, ask the *aiterway* if we can order some *alettegays* with *eglay* of *orkpay*.'

He slapped the table and burst out laughing.

'Stop messing around, George, you know perfectly well the *waiter* doesn't have any *galettes* with *leg of pork*.'

That shut George up. He stared at Charles in surprise. Charles liked the idea of pig Latin, it made his brain work hard, and that was no bad thing these days.

The waiter started to laugh as well.

'What kind of language is that you're speaking? If you like, we can speak Breton!'

'No thanks, I think we've had enough for now. Right, we'll take two *galettes*, a *fermière* and a *Chavignol*, please.'

'But while we're on the subject of foreign languages, Monsieur—' George cut in.

'Oh, because Breton is a foreign language, is it?' said the waiter, outraged. 'And in Brest, of all places!'

'Sorry, sorry! My apologies. But might there be some young person here who can speak text language?'

'Oh yes, we've got an expert here, Alexandre. If you'll wait a moment, I'll get him for you. Alexandre!'

'Alexandre, send through an order for two *galettes*, a *fermière* and a *Chavignol*, and then would you kindly explain to these gentlemen – as quickly as possible, mind, you've got other things to be getting on with – how to use text language?'

Young Alexandre, a blond boy of about twenty with a whisper of a moustache, stiffly gelled hair and a piercing in one ear, answered shyly:

'Well, you don't have to know text language to—'

'Yes, yes, I know,' interrupted George, 'but if you write it the way you're meant to, you know, swoosh.' He gestured vaguely with his arms. 'We want to learn, so show us.'

The young waiter perched on the end of the banquette and took hold of the biro hanging around his neck.

'So, the point of the whole thing is to shorten words as much as possible. So, like, "How are you?" would be "hw r u", you see?'

He wrote 'hw r u' on the paper tablecloth.

'So, in a text, you'd know that means "How are you?".'

'You mean, the point is to leave out vowels?' said George.

Alexandre thought for a moment.

'Actually, not always. You've just got to shorten the word as much as possible. So, um, OK, you can leave out letters, or you can write with numbers. For example, the "one" sound can be written with a figure "1" and the "to" sound with a figure "2", and so on.'

'OK, let me give it a go,' said George. 'Let's see ... "I've gone to a restaurant in Brest".' Then he wrote on the tablecloth: 'Iv gon 2 a restaurant in Brest'.

'I would have put *a Brest restaurant*,' Charles pointed out. 'Then it's even shorter.'

George shot his friend a disapproving glare. Alexandre seemed more enthusiastic now, and grabbed the pen from George to correct the sentence.

'But you can make it even shorter.'

He crossed out George's words and wrote:

'iv gon 2 a rstrnt in Brest.'

Another waiter appeared.

'What are you all doing?'

'We're writing text messages,' George replied.

'On a tablecloth? I'm not sure they'll get very far! Ha!'

Ignoring the joke, George studied the sentence, frowning.

'OK, I see. Well, "rstrnt" doesn't sound as nice as "rest-aurrant", but OK, if it works better ...'

'So, the most important thing,' said Alexandre, 'is that you now have more space to write other things. You're always trying to save on each word so you can put as many as possible in the text.'

'That's just where you're wrong, young man. I save for the sake of saving!' George exclaimed.

'Alexandre,' Charles interrupted. 'Show us another example, so we're sure we know how to do it. We don't want to make any mistakes!'

So Alexandre carried on the lesson.

'OK, let's say: "I'm going to have dessert at the restaurant".'

'No,' said Charles. 'Why don't you say: "I'm going to have dessert here". Because we already know how to write "restaurant".'

Alexandre leaned over the tablecloth, which by this point was covered in scribbles, and started writing. When he sat up again, George and Charles saw: 'Im goin 2 hav dessert here.'

'It doesn't look that much shorter than the normal version,' Charles said, suspiciously.

'Isn't there a text word for "dessert"?'

'Not that I can think of, off the top of my head.'

Alexandre crossed out the word several times on the tablecloth, adding and taking away letters, before finally admitting defeat: 'dessert' was just 'dessert'.

'OK, so "dessert" doesn't really work. But you probably won't use that word very much anyway; I mean, how often do you write texts about dessert? But there are loads of words that we use all the time that you can make much shorter.'

'For example?' asked Charles.

Alexandre thought again.

'I know! "Speak tomorrow". You write that all the time.'

'Yes!' exclaimed George. 'I'm going to use that one every day!'

Alexandre wrote 'spk 2moro' and looked at the two pensioners with an air of satisfaction.

'Look, I saved five characters just like that! OK, it doesn't sound like that much, but—'

'Yes, it does, you've saved almost fifty per cent! Bravo, young man! Let's have another one.'

'Hmm, I don't know … Oh wait, that's perfect! "I don't know".'

He wrote 'I dno'.

'Hmm, I'm not sure how much we're going to be needing that one,' objected Charles. 'Especially as we'll be following the map all the way.'

'OK, I've got a better one! "Want to". You use that all the time, right?'

'Ah yes,' agreed George. 'One of the modal verbs, very common.'

'OK, check this out: "wan2".'

'Waan two?'

'No! "Wan" plus "2" makes "want to"!'

This time, George and Charles were really impressed. Alexandre felt pleased with himself.

'And I saved three characters, including a space, which isn't bad either.'

'Well, would you look at that! Right, Charles old chap, we'd better get started ... And that's all very well, young Alexandre, but have you ever heard someone speak pig Latin?'

Alexandre had not, but by the end of the evening, with the help of some local cider, he could speak it fluently, along with the rest of the kitchen staff and quite a few of the other diners, and the restaurant resounded with all kinds of *onsensenay*. At around one in the morning, they ran out of Breton songs to sing, so George brought out some of the classics: Maurice Chevalier, Ouvrard, Milton ... But when he was the only one left singing, everyone decided it was time to go home.

Adèle was bored. She spent all her time waiting around. Whether on her own or with the crew, day or night, she waited. There was no way she could leave this musty old house and go and stretch her legs in Brick Lane. If someone shouted her name, it was her job to appear instantly. It was impossible for her to read, or start a crossword, or anything; she just had to wait around and try her best to look interested.

Once again she found herself sitting in a corridor with a few other crew members. It was a different corridor this time, one that led to the large drawing room, but it was just as gloomy, with the same velvet curtains cloaked in dust and the same old windows that let in draughts.

The drawing room, where the scene was being shot, was big enough to have allowed her to find a small space for herself in the warm and at the heart of the action, but at the last minute someone had sent her off to find a prop and she hadn't been able to get back in as filming had already started. They had obviously decided they didn't need what they had sent her off to get. Adèle sighed and sat down on the floor. In the corridor, the assistant electricians were talking with the lorry drivers who had come in to grab a coffee. Two actors who had gone through make-up hours ago were pacing up and down and going over their lines. The assistant hairdresser was clearly still hung-over from the night before and was sitting slumped on the stairs. Adèle looked at her watch for the umpteenth time: 11.12 p.m. At least another two hours before she could go home. She yawned, then switched on her phone. Oh joy, one voicemail and three texts. That would eat up at least a few minutes. All of the texts were from her grandfather.

Grandpa 28/09/2008 19:02

We r in a rstrnt in Brest, Finstr. We r fine.

(We're in a restaurant in Brest, Finistère. We're fine.)

Grandpa 28/09/2008 20:58

Still in St-Malo rstrnt. V gd chavignol galett n strwbry crep. V nice atmsphr. Spking pig latin like in gd old days. Spk 2moro.

(Still in Saint-Malo restaurant. Very good *Chavignol galette* and strawberry crêpes. Very nice atmosphere. Speaking pig Latin like in the good old days. Speak tomorrow.)

Grandpa 28/09/2008 21:09

Rstrnt is in Brest, bt called Crepri St-Malo. Spk 2moro.

(Restaurant is in Brest, but called Crêperie Saint-Malo. Speak tomorrow.)

Adèle couldn't stop herself from smiling.

The voicemail was also from her grandfather and had been received at seven minutes to eleven – which meant seven minutes to midnight in France. What was he doing up at that hour and why was he calling her? It was with some trepidation that she pressed play. She listened to the sound of noisy laughter and waited for the message that never came. Her grandfather had dialled her number by mistake and what she was hearing was the background noise of the crêperie. It did sound quite fun there, actually. She was about to erase the message when she picked out the sound of men's voices singing 'Jean-Françoué de Nantes … Jean-Françoué' and then 'The Bretons know how to have a good time!' That was definitely her grandfather's voice.

Adèle laughed to herself. If this was stage one, they were going to have to be treated for alcohol poisoning by the time they reached the end of the Tour. This man matched up less and less to the image of her grandfather she had in her mind. When she was little, she had been given a 'Grandpa Kiki', the grandpa version of the soft toy monkey that had been such a craze in the eighties. Grandpa Kiki was grey all over, with glasses, a three-piece suit and a pair of carpet slippers. Since then, she had always pictured her grandfather as a Grandpa Kiki, who just sat in his box, and whom she would send the occasional card out of habit and politeness. And here he was jumping out of his box at the age of eighty-three! Grandpa Kiki dancing *Saturday Night Fever*? The mental image made her smile.

Adèle liked getting these texts; they distracted her from the monotony of the shoot. She looked up and saw that Alex, the apprentice hair stylist, was watching her. He was tall and slim, and most likely gay. Like many of the Australians she knew, he was friendly and laid-back, and loved going out. He must have been wondering why she was grinning in the middle of all these people who looked like they were about to die of boredom.

Adèle whispered:

'I just got a text from my grandfather, he's eighty-three. Apparently he's sitting in a crêperie in Brittany knocking back cider. I wouldn't be surprised if he was dancing on the tables by now.'

'So your grandfather's in pretty good shape, then!'

'No, not even! That's the crazy thing about it. Everyone said he was on his last legs. But I haven't told you the funniest part: he's been surgically attached to his slippers for twenty years and now all of a sudden he decides he's going to do the Tour de France.'

'The Tour de France? On a bike?'

'No, in a Renault Scenic. But still ...'

Adèle briefly summed up the story for him, not without a hint of pride. They carried on whispering and laughing under their breath until the cast and crew came out of the drawing room more than two hours later. They talked about their misguided hopes, all the unbearable waiting, how hard it was to make real friends, how cynical the industry was – but they also discussed their future plans, eccentric relatives, holidays in Brittany and faraway countries. There was a little gossip, but this time Adèle found it funny. It was the first time since her conversations with Irving Ferns that she had opened up to someone on set. And even if she never saw Alex again, this hadn't been a bad evening at all.

When George returned to his room in the Hôtel du Centre, the walls were no longer the urine-yellow and concrete-grey of the night before; they now looked like sunshine and soft grey cashmere. The room was no longer anonymous, but welcoming. Beyond the uPVC window, the night was filled with future promise, with things that had long lain dormant but were coming back to life, full of energy and vigour. The source of this unexpected jubilance was, amongst other things, the memory of a baby girl in a maternity ward twenty-three years earlier, and his joy at being a grandfather for the first time. But a whole host of other thoughts were also contributing to his happiness as he sat down on his bed.

George had been an atheist, and occasional opponent of the Church, ever since his catechism lessons with Père François some seventy years ago. So what was behind this sudden urge to thank someone who was not an actual person? Someone who would understand and who knew where he came from, someone who made the rain fall and the sun shine, who had control of his body and the events that affected him. All his life he had avoided churches; he was not the sort to go asking God favours. He, or perhaps Arlette, was the ship's captain, and he never asked anyone, not the Father, the Son or the Holy Ghost, for anything (even if Arlette, he knew, had occasionally done so in secret, especially towards the end). And after all, he had lived no worse a life than most, far from it. And yet in these moments it was tempting to be grateful to someone other than his own pile of flesh and bones, which, he mistakenly thought, hadn't been responsible for any of it. He was content and grateful. He had to admit, there was something straightforward and cheering about thanking the angels, in whom he had never believed, but who existed that evening just to share in his new-found happiness.

The next morning, he felt the full effects of the night's good cheer.

Monday 29 September

Brest (Finistère)–Guémené-sur-Scorff (Morbihan)

George and Charles reconvened the following morning in the hotel breakfast room. There was no avoiding it: they were both hung-over. Charles was groaning and complaining, while George was trying as hard as humanly possible to hide his discomfort. In the buffet area, the appetising aroma of the pastries mingled with waves of woody aftershave and a heavy dose of lady's perfume. The guests approached the buffet as if walking on stage, shyly muttering, 'Morning, morning', and standing up very straight. They all put on their best manners, neatly cutting the cheese and taking care not to overfill their plates, fighting off the desire to try everything and make the most of the 'all-you-can-eat' buffet. Charles and George, on the other hand, were not concerned in the slightest with keeping up appearances, especially in the absence of their wives, and piled their plates high with bread and cheese – which admittedly looked a little plastic, but would do the job fine.

Once they had devoured their breakfast, Charles said:

'You know, I thought for a moment there we weren't going to do it, George. But here we are: stage one of the Tour de France. And with a stinking hangover to boot! I have to say, I didn't see that one coming.'

'Maybe it would be a good idea to wait until after lunch before we get back on the road,' George suggested tentatively.

'Out of the question! I've been waiting until *after lunch* for forty years to do this bloody Tour. Come on, let's go!'

The first morning of the Tour was chilly but stunning. The sun was shining over Brittany, and if the photographs in Charles's guidebooks were anything to go by, the landscape promised to be wild and full of mystery.

George and Charles allowed themselves a few detours, to see the countryside and give them some stories to tell in the postcards.

The rhythm of the epic journey had been set: it was to be a stroll, rather than a sprint. So they spent the first day discovering the lovely Plougastel peninsula, with its grey stone chapels, impressive calvary and L'Auberlac'h, the tiny shellfish port lined with little blue boats, which was so charming that George felt a surge of poetic inspiration. It was perhaps a little early for the evening text, given that they hadn't even eaten lunch yet, but there was nothing wrong with reassuring Adèle in the morning as well. Just in case she had had a sudden worry overnight. George got out his mobile and wrote:

We r in L'Auberlac'h, Fnstr, nice port w blu boats.
(We are in L'Auberlac'h, Finistère, nice port with blue boats.)

He tried to think of a shorthand for 'boats' but didn't want to confuse Adèle, so he left it as it was. The response came almost immediately.

OK, hv fun.
(OK, have fun.)

George really did find the little port rather charming.

They did not talk much about the Tour during this stage. George tried to start a game where the aim was to name the years in which Breton cyclists had stood out from the pack. A good half-hour had gone by before George realised that he was winning by miles and that Charles's only contribution was the occasional 'Ah', 'Ah yes, you're right.' George, on the other hand, surpassed himself: he had remembered Jean-Marie Goasmat, known as 'The Elf'; Alfred Le Bars and his journey from Morlaix to Paris; the 'Bulldog of Morbihan', Le Guilly; Malléjac, the factory worker from Brest who took the yellow jersey in '53; George Gilles, of course (the 'Breton Van Steenbergen'); 'La Pipe' and his Mercier bike; the Groussard brothers; 'Jo Talbot'; Ronan Pensec with his mane of hair (with a name like his, he could only be from around these parts), and so on and so forth. George reproached Charles for his lack of enthusiasm, but he replied that he was concentrating on the road, and couldn't do two things at once. So that was the end of that.

The countryside they were driving through was magnificent. The lanes wound through a sea of green, passing grey chapels and little fishing villages tucked away in deserted bays, and every so often at a bend in the narrow, bracken-lined roads, they caught breathtaking views over the Bay of Brest. Signs along the way reminded them that they were crossing Armorica Regional Park, and pointed to rows of standing stones. Armorica, and the menhirs ... This brought back memories for George, who had read the Asterix stories to Adèle when she was a little girl.

When the road took them through thick forest, they had the strange feeling of being caught somewhere between day and night. And that if they ventured to look further beyond the trees, they might have seen something, a something that only existed in fairy tales. They went from rocky landscapes to purple heaths, to rutted tracks and, further on, empty expanses of peatland.

It wasn't time for lunch yet, but Charles wanted to stop in Le Faou. George naively assumed he wanted to see the old houses, and the pretty port with its mud flats. Not at all; Charles kept driving until they reached a wisteria-covered farm at the very edge of the village. Apparently, this was where the best cider in the region was to be found. George, who was still feeling a little nauseous, wondered aloud if this was really necessary, and stayed in the car. Charles and the owner returned with two crates, which they placed in the Scenic's spacious boot.

It would soon be time for the first official lunch of the Tour. George grabbed the guidebook from the glove compartment and began to read:

'So, the Black Mountains. Let's see. Blah blah blah sixty kilometres blah blah blah Le Ménez-Hom blah blah blah blah blah dense forest blah blah blah blah schist blah blah blah blah blah blah blah three hundred million years blah blah blah blah hidden charm blah blah blah slate blah blah blah blah. Right. None of that tells us where to take a pit stop.'

'Look up Châteauneuf-du-Faou, we'll be there soon,' advised Charles.

Châteauneuf-du-Faou was a pretty market town perched on a hillside in the Black Mountains. The pair found a picnic area in the grounds of the Trévarez estate, one of the prettiest parks in Brittany. They took the picnic set out of the car, along with the crate of tomatoes and the provisions picked up at a corner shop in Brest. They both took out their old Opinel knives. The château ruins, the verdant riverbanks and the tranquillity of the place inspired George to write another text. He hesitated for a moment before sending it: it wouldn't do to send too many ... but anyway, a text was never a nuisance and didn't necessarily require a response. Even if George did love receiving them from Adèle.

We r in Chateauneuf-du-Faou, nice twn, picnic w breton cidr.

(We are in Châteauneuf-du-Faou, nice town, picnic with Breton cider.)

They got up to leave when they saw dark clouds gathering on the horizon. Charles, who was normally extremely conscientious, sometimes even obsessively so, surprised George by leaving his leftovers on the immaculate lawn. As he got back into the car, seemingly unaware, George picked up his rubbish for him, grumbling under his breath. How funny that even after thirty years, he still did not really know his neighbour.

In Guémené, they had dinner in a little restaurant that offered regional specialities. But the trials of the Tour – and the high jinks of the night before – had left them both exhausted. They were in danger of falling asleep into the Kirs they had ordered to mark the occasion, more out of a sense of duty than fun. They soon ran out of jokes about Guémené, the hometown of *andouille* sausage, and at half past nine the companions were lying in their respective rooms in their striped pyjamas, in a bed and breakfast that Charles had booked online. George sent a last text to Adèle and noticed that '*andouille*', like 'dessert', was difficult to abbreviate in text language. And as his doctor had banned him from eating pork anyway, he decided to omit this detail from his message.

We r in Guémené-sur-Scorff, luvly cttage, nice frnt. Rstrnt w rejonal spcialities, 2 end a lng day. Celebr8d 1st stage of tour w Kir. 2moro Plumelec, lnch in Guern. Gd nite Adl.

(We are in Guémené-sur-Scorff, lovely cottage, nice front. Restaurant with regional specialities, to end a long day. Celebrated first stage of Tour with Kir. Tomorrow Plumelec, lunch in Guern. Goodnight Adèle.)

He pressed 'send' just before turning off the bedside lamp

around 10 p.m., and fell asleep straight away. Apart from the obligatory 4 a.m. loo trip, it was a long and peaceful night's sleep. Which was lucky, because in the days to come he would not sleep anything like as soundly …

Tuesday 30 September

Guémené-sur-Scorff–Plumelec (Morbihan)

The second part of this first stage of the Tour was just as pleasant, interesting and exhausting. They stopped for a picnic of *andouille* and cider by the cemetery in Guern, next to the village fountain, where the music of the falling water inspired another text to Adèle, which also went unanswered, but George understood that his granddaughter was very busy.

They reached Plumelec, where a charming bed and breakfast awaited them. This time Charles and George would have to share a bedroom, which was furnished with twin beds with white crochet bedcovers and a cushion with a yellow knitted cover embroidered with flowers.

For dinner they opted, like teenagers, for a takeaway pizza from a pizza van that came to the town's church square every Tuesday. Charles, who had been put in charge of ordering, chose one pizza for them to share, as they were not very hungry – perhaps because of their excessive sausage consumption earlier that afternoon. When Charles came to choosing toppings, the pizza man began to miss his teenage customers. Charles didn't garnish his pizza so much as pile it high with every possible ingredient. Most of the available toppings were heaped onto the poor thing, which inevitably crumbled under the great weight. They needed an extra box just to catch the excess spilling over the sides. The pizza man would not forget these two granddads; as for George and Charles, they were delighted with the result.

Before going to bed, George sent a last text to Adèle:

We r in Plumelec, in Chouan country. Pizza 4 dinr, Charles snds his luv, me 2. Gd nite Adl.

(We are in Plumelec, in Chouan country. Pizza for dinner, Charles sends his love and me too. Goodnight Adèle.)

Charles was leaning on the sunflower-yellow cushion and concentrating hard on his *Sudoku – Holiday Special*, his knife-sharpened pencil in hand. George was impressed; he was so tired he hadn't even had the energy to pick up his book. They started chatting, and continued their conversation after they had turned the lights out like the boys in boarding-house dormitories they had once been.

And neither he nor Charles woke up when the phone played the little jingle signalling the arrival of a text message, just before eleven. A text that was not from Adèle.

Meanwhile, around nine o'clock, Adèle was coming to the end

of a long day that had begun at six in the morning. She hadn't had time to respond to the last text from her grandfather as there had just been some bad news that had cast a dark cloud over the whole crew, and turned the shooting schedule on its head. His agent had called the producer late that afternoon: Irving Ferns was dead. The actor who had played Aristide Leonides, the murdered grandfather, had passed away in the night at the age of eighty-one. The producers were now tearing their hair out because even though they had already shot the opening scene with him, he had been supposed to reappear in a flashback that was scheduled to be shot next week. So they not only had to find a replacement for the scenes still to be shot, but also for the ones in which he had already appeared. For the production manager, this was catastrophic: there was no budget for this, blah blah blah, they would have to recreate the scene and décor exactly, blah blah blah, costumes made to measure, blah blah blah, moustache continuity, blah blah blah ... For Adèle, and for most of the crew, this meant a few extra days of shooting. And she had thought she would have a day off on her birthday ... Not any more! But above all, the actor's death had deeply upset her.

She was the last person to collect her things in the crooked house. The place was quite eerie when it was empty, with dark walls and a creaking floor. She had to lock the front door and give the key to the porter down the road. She couldn't stop thinking about Irving Ferns. Would she send flowers? She had only known him for two days, but she had been shocked by his death. She had sensed that he had felt alone and that he would have liked to continue their conversation, open up more. But Adèle had not wanted to confide in him. He had been the reason she had called her grandfather for the first time in years. Contrary to what her grandpa seemed to think, her mother had never asked her to do anything. But Irving Ferns had.

She looked at her phone. So many messages from her grandfather! At least five a day. He told her all about the trip, the villages he passed through and the countryside he was seeing. He was going way beyond the daily update she had asked for; this was more like a travel diary. She read his texts as if they were the logbook of an explorer. It gave her a chance to escape a little.

But Irving Ferns' death helped her see these little text messages for what they really were. They weren't a travel diary, written for her, the reader, with the sole purpose of keeping her entertained. They were an invitation to start a dialogue between a distant grandfather and an absent granddaughter. Up until now, Adèle had always unknowingly refused this invitation. And this was probably her last chance to accept.

She reread all of the texts, which she now saw in a different light, more faded and melancholy. Because most of them had not been replied to, they now seemed to contain a sadness that she hadn't noticed before. She was struck by her own selfishness, the egotism of youth, just as she had been after her conversation with the ageing actor.

And so, once again, she decided to try to make up for lost time.

A few hundred kilometres away, in Brittany, George was also wide awake. The night had begun well but his bladder had woken him up, as it always did, around four in the morning. It was then that he realised he had forgotten to pack an essential item in his suitcase: a torch. It was pitch-black in the room and he didn't want to switch on the bedside light and wake up Charles. In a flash of inspiration he remembered that the mobile phone lit up when the buttons were pressed. Feeling his way, he found the phone and pressed a few buttons so he could make his way to the bathroom without stirring Charles. He paid no attention to the distant ringing noise he could hear. He thought it was probably the plumbing. It was only when he put the phone back on the bedside table and was about to pull the cover over him that he heard: 'Hello? Hello, George?' George grabbed his phone and was horrified to see 'Ginette Bruneau' on the screen. He had obviously woken her up. Mortified, he pressed as many of the buttons as he could until finally the talking stopped. He was relieved for a moment until the panic returned: if he knew it was Ginette he had called, then Ginette must have known it was him who had hung up on her in the middle of the night. This would worry her, no doubt about that. How had the blasted thing managed to find Ginette's number of all things? Stupid blasted machine.

He went back into the bathroom to call Ginette back to reassure her, but before he dialled the number, he saw that he had received a text. From Ginette.

Ginette Bruneau 30/09/2008 22:49

Dear George, I am thinking of you both on your journey. I won a lovely begonia in the dance contest for the Charleston; it was a lot of fun. Maybe one day you'll be able to come to one of the dances. I hope you are doing well. Yours, Ginette.

George did not call her back. This was an extremely delicate situation. He had to think about it, and not rush into anything. And most importantly, he mustn't say a word of this to Charles. For even if it had been sent at a perfectly reasonable hour, Ginette's message gave cause for secrecy.

Wednesday 1 October

Plumelec–Auray (Morbihan)

The next day was a one-off: they drove all the way to the next destination without stopping. They arrived before lunchtime. The hotel, which was situated in a clearing on the outskirts of Auray, was magnificent. It was refined without being pretentious, with discreet service, antique décor and plush carpets. Guests watched the rain battering the trees from the comfort of the winter garden. Their lunch was utterly delicious. It was the most beautiful place they had stayed yet.

George was overcome with the desire to relax, to collapse into one of the great wicker sofas that looked so inviting, a perfect place for contemplation and reflection, but Charles was not to be persuaded. They had left the afternoon free to visit the world-famous Carnac site. Charles had been saying since the beginning of the trip that what he really wanted to see in Brittany was Carnac, with the Louison Bobet Cycling Museum a close second.

No matter the weather, Charles was determined to get out there. George also wanted to see the Carnac standing stones, of course, but the driving rain was enough to make his rheumatism play up just thinking about it. In the end, Charles's determination won out against George's rheumatism, and George pulled on the red fleece that Françoise had given him. They got back into the Scenic and set off for Carnac.

From the car they could already see some of the stone alignments but they would have to walk much further to take in the sheer scale of the three thousand menhirs, dolmens and tumulus that Charles had heard so much about. But the rain had turned into a deluge, and leaving the car now was out of the question. So they waited in the car park by the town hall, and waited some more, for at least an hour, but the water continued to flood the windscreen. George had to bite his tongue not to mention Ginette, which he did for so long that he fell asleep. After a while Charles shook George awake and suggested they go and visit the Museum of Prehistory on the square. From the car, they could see the large white classical stone building with its impressive doorway and a palm tree in the courtyard that was being pulled here and there by the wind.

George had always found museums rather boring. Not that he wasn't interested in culture or history. He had an excellent memory for facts, and his general knowledge was superb. But there was something profoundly, fundamentally, soporific about museums. He felt bored to death just at the thought of dragging himself down dimly lit corridors and pressing his head against the glass to read the Lilliputian print on the information panels. The first thing he did, as he had done every other time he was made to visit a museum, was to find a bench to sit down on. There were always benches in museums, and they always had old people lined up on them, like sparrows on a wire. There were always clusters of teenagers as well, hanging around in their trainers and talking loudly. George watched them. He knew these snot-nosed kids on a class trip, who couldn't care less about prehistory, found it pathetic how old people did nothing but wait around on benches. But what the sniggering youths didn't know was that the old man in the red fleece was planning what to write in a text to his new girl. That would have knocked them for six! George chuckled to himself on his bench.

Charles returned, having enjoyed the exhibition, and bought at least five books on the stone rows at the museum shop. George asked the woman at the till if it was possible to buy a torch here but she patiently replied that no, surprisingly enough, the Museum of Prehistory gift shop did not sell flashlights. They went back to the hotel where, finally, George was able to collapse onto a wicker sofa.

Thursday 2 October

Auray (Morbihan)–Mûr-de-Bretagne (Côtes-d'Armor)

Things became difficult when Charles saw the bill for their stay. Never had the question 'What's the damage?' been so appropriate. What he had thought was the total price at the time of booking turned out to be the price per person without breakfast. With taxes, all the other extras and the two lunches, the total cost was staggering and he was in a black mood by the time it came to paying. Or rather, by the time it came to asking George to pay, as George was this Tour's sole sponsor, and while he had been incredibly generous when it came to the main expenses, for anything that might be considered an 'extra' he kept his purse strings drawn rather tight. By some miracle he was in an excellent mood that day and paid the full amount without hesitation, and even gave the receptionist a big smile as he did so.

Admittedly, he had just been pleasantly surprised by a text from Adèle on his screen:

Adèle 01/10/2008 22:36

Alwys wnted 2 c Carnac. If u giv me the name of htel, mayb ill go 1 day, u nvr no! Spk 2moro.

(Always wanted to see Carnac. If you give me the name of the hotel, maybe I'll go one day, you never know! Speak tomorrow.)

If the family was going to come back here, it was probably a good idea to smile at the receptionist.

Charles was eager to visit Auray, where he had been with Thérèse many years earlier. The summer tourists had all left and this little corner of Brittany was just as beautiful as he remembered. The town sat majestically on top of a hill, with the old port, Saint-Goustan, at the foot of it. Charles and George walked down Rue du Belvédère, with its terraced gardens and medieval houses, until they reached the banks of the Loch. They stopped in the shade of some large trees to take in the stunning view of the port. They could even see the watchtower that saw the ships in every day. They walked for a long time, panting as they climbed the steep streets and uneven steps that led to the church, totally forgetting to buy a torch for George, even though he had kept going on about it. Finally, the exhausted visitors were grateful to sit down on the terrace of a restaurant with purple walls and striped sofas. By now they should have been in Baud, or even in Pontivy, about sixty kilometres from where they were, but never mind.

George started to compose another text to Adèle. Ever the 'text message minstrel' (Charles's expression), he sang the praises of Auray, and recommended various attractions for her potential holiday in the region. A few passers-by smiled at the sight of the granddad frantically texting on the terrace of a hip restaurant.

Adèle responded soon afterwards; filming was going well, but she was tired. George read the message aloud to Charles, not without a surge of pride, and said that she worked too hard. They had a large lunch and took their time over it. They would head straight for the next hotel after lunch, which was in Mûr-de-Bretagne, eighty kilometres away. After a starter, main, dessert, coffee, and post-coffee liqueur, they walked slowly back to the car and left Auray.

Just after they had left the town, and Charles was calmly driving onwards, comforted by the soothing sounds of the GPS, George suddenly yelled:

'There! TURN!'

Charles yanked the wheel, narrowly missing the flower barrow in the middle of the roundabout, almost crushing the car on his left, scraping the one on his right, knocking over a signpost and driving into a trolley that had been left at the side of the road. Miraculously they came away more shaken than actually hurt, but at least three cars honked furiously at them. Charles in turn yelled at George.

'What in God's name was that for?'

'I just saw a supermarket! The torch!'

'What? You almost made us crash because of a bloody torch? This torch thing is becoming an obsession, it's really getting on my nerves now!'

'But I need one by this evening! It might be the only supermarket for miles!'

George was getting worked up too; this was the first time in thirty years that he had been told off by his neighbour.

'But why do you need it right now, can't it wait?'

'No, it can't wait! Because I'm telling you now, I'm fed up of calling your sister every time I need to take a piss!'

'Huh?'

George had slammed the door of the Scenic and was already running towards the shopping centre. Utterly perplexed, Charles stayed in the car, both hands gripping the steering wheel.

The atmosphere was strained when George returned to the car; they were like a young couple after their first spat. George did not deign to offer an explanation of the link between Ginette, his bladder and the torch, but Charles wisely decided it was best to leave it.

At 5 p.m. they were still only in Baud, about halfway. The Scenic was parked three hundred metres from the village's only tourist attraction, the Fountain of Clarity, with its old washbowl. But the fountain and washbowl were not destined to go down amongst the glorious memories of the Tour: Charles and George were fast asleep in the car. The meal in Auray and the incident in the supermarket car park had caught up with them.

They got back on the road in the late afternoon and drove all the way to Mûr-de-Bretagne without stopping in Pontivy, although they could make out the two sides to the city as they passed through it: the imperial part, dominated by geometric lines and elegant structures, and the medieval heart of the city, characterised by narrow winding streets lined with timber-framed houses. They passed the dead-straight canal, and then they were out in the countryside again, as the sun was setting.

Just before reaching Mûr-de-Bretagne, they stopped at a service station. George bought a battery for his torch in the shop – it was shameful that the torch hadn't come with any, and what was more, he knew he had some at home. When he came out of the shop, George saw that something wasn't right. Charles was standing exactly where he had left him five minutes earlier, staring at the petrol pump.

'So did you fill it up, then?'

Charles said he hadn't. He looked at George with a dazed expression and got back into the car. Annoyed, George seized the pump and filled the tank. They drove to the next bed and breakfast in complete silence.

It was a large stone house typical of the area, which would later be described by George in a text to Adèle: there was a skylight in the steep slate roof, three walls without any windows, just small openings, a chimney in every gable, an outdoor staircase with worn steps, and finally, in the courtyard amid the rose bushes, a clay bread oven.

They had a light supper in the spacious living area and then retired to the room they were sharing. They were both aware that close proximity encourages confidences, and that at some point they were going to have to talk about the link between the torch and Ginette.

Just as they were about to turn off their bedside lights, Charles broke the silence that was weighing heavily in the air:

'OK, George, this thing about my sister, well ...'

'Oh yes, your sister. I'd forgotten about that.'

'I mean ... why did you need to buy the torch?'

George summed up the Guémené incident, and then read him Ginette's text message.

'And that's all?' asked Charles.

'Yes, that's all.'

'Oh, that's alright then. Because I've got to say, I wasn't quite sure what to make of what you said at the supermarket.'

'It just came out like that, I was in shock, we'd just had an accident, or as good as.'

'Yes, thanks for reminding me! And whose fault was that? Anyway, never mind. So how are you going to reply to that?'

'Dunno. I've been thinking about it for two days, but I don't know what to say.'

'Want my opinion?'

'Yes,' lied George.

'Reply to the text when you've got something to say.' He paused for emphasis and then carried on:

'Believe me. Talking to women when really you've got nothing to say to them never did anyone any good. And I'm not saying that just because she's my sister.'

'You know, that's not bad advice,' said George, actually quite impressed.

'Well, there you go.'

'But she's not going to be offended or anything?'

'Oh!' exclaimed Charles. 'I can't help you at all there. Psychology's not really my strong point.'

Now that everything was out in the open, the mood lightened considerably. Charles got out his Sudoku and George began writing a text to Adèle describing the house. He got a reply a few minutes later:

Adèle 02/10/2008 22:46

Luky u, id rther b in brttany thn in ldn. we r shooting crooked house by Agatha Christie in a v old, dark crooked house + v bad wthr here. Heres 2 brttany!

(Lucky you, I'd rather be in Brittany than in London. We are shooting *Crooked House* by Agatha Christie in a very old, dark and crooked house and very bad weather here. Here's to Brittany!)

George smiled and made a note to buy a copy of the book the next day. He felt excited about the day to come, just as he had always done as a young boy.

Friday 3 October

Mûr-de-Bretagne–Saint-Brieuc (Côtes-d'Armor)

When George woke up, Charles was already getting dressed. It was not even eight yet; George asked him what was going on.

'I was thinking of going to the market. I talked to the lady at reception yesterday, apparently there's a little market in the village that sells local produce. Farmer's cider, foie gras, goat's cheese, everything. Not to be missed, she said. So, would you rather stay in bed or are you coming?'

'Oh no, I'll let you go. My back's playing up again; this bed is too soft.'

In fact, the bed was fine, and his back, for once, was not bothering him at all. But George felt like a rest. This Tour was turning out to be pretty exhausting. Today he would have a lie-in.

But he hadn't counted on Charles having quite so much energy. As soon as he came back from the market he was talking about getting back in the car to go and visit the hydroelectric dam in Guerlédan, not far from there. George, who had only just finished his breakfast, began by dragging his feet, but the beautiful countryside bathed in autumn sunlight was enough to revive his enthusiasm. It seemed almost as though they were in Switzerland, surrounded as they were by valleys and craggy forested peaks criss-crossed with walking trails. The dam had created a magnificent lake in the heart of the forest. Charles and George picnicked on a feast from the market in the shade cast by the ruins of Bon-Repos abbey, and George, inspired once again by the beauty of his surroundings, sent a long message to Adèle.

In the afternoon they followed the Tour itinerary – the beautiful old houses at Corlay, the town of Châtelaudren on the river Leff, Plérin with its beaches and sandy coves beneath towering cliffs – and got to Hotel Regina in Saint-Brieuc before nightfall.

From the bay, George wrote to Adèle:

St Brieuc Bay: luvly beach, ntr rsrv, wndrful lndscape, amzing cliffs, little ports in the roks. St Brieuc has lots of chrming little sts, old houses, nice shops. This eve we r eatin mussls. u hav 2 come here wen ur in Brttny. 2moro goin 2 buy agatha kristi bk 2 kno wat hppens @ the end! luv.

(Saint-Brieuc Bay: lovely beach, nature reserve, wonderful landscape, amazing cliffs, little ports in the rocks. Saint-Brieuc has lots of charming little streets, old houses, nice shops. This evening we're eating mussels. You have to come here when you're in Brittany. Tomorrow I'm going to buy the Agatha Christie book to know what happens at the end! Love.)

Adèle replied:

Not hard 2 guess wat happens @ end. let me kno wat u think of bk. I think not best AC. I prfr and then there were none.

(Not hard to guess what happens at the end. Let me know what you think of the book. I think not the best Agatha Christie. I prefer *And Then There Were None*.)

Come evening, George couldn't resist texting back:

Prfr classic: mrdr on orient xpress. cnt w8 2 read crkd house. hotel in st brieuc awful, loud ppl evrywer. gd nite.

(Prefer a classic: *Murder on the Orient Express*. Can't wait to read *Crooked House*. Hotel in Saint-Brieuc awful, loud people everywhere. Goodnight.)

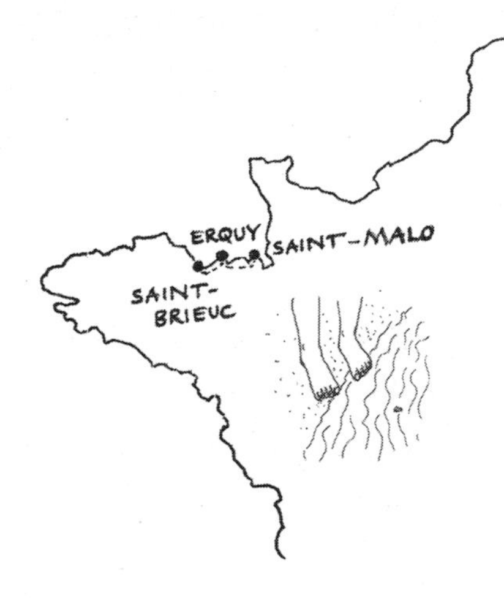

Saturday 4 October

Saint-Brieuc (Côtes-d'Armor)–Saint-Malo (Ille-et-Vilaine)

The next morning, George was in a foul mood. He began by complaining about his bedroom, then about the breakfast room, which was too cold, too large and too quiet. George thought of family breakfasts in the days when they all still saw each other regularly, with Arlette, Françoise, her husband, and little Adèle. The kitchen would be filled with the smell of toast and coffee, and the sound of everyone talking. But even at home on his own, breakfast was a noisy affair: the sound of the coffee machine, the stove heating up, the radio in the background, the pop of the toaster. Here everyone spoke in a whisper, and blushed if by accident they made any noise.

Another reason George found the room depressing was because the lights had been turned on at eight in the morning. Large dark clouds were gathering in the grey sky, making the streets of Saint-Brieuc look almost forbidding. They had become used to the pleasant and sunny early October weather, but winter was clearly descending upon them and was already making his joints ache.

'The weather's turning.'

'Mmm,' replied Charles, who was sipping his own green tea that he brought to breakfast every morning.

'Can't you feel it? My joints are stiff again; I don't think that's a good sign.'

'Oh, it'll be fine. The weather changes all the time in Brittany, you know. In the morning the weather's foul and by the afternoon you're sunning yourself on the beach.'

'Mmm,' said George, not convinced.

A little break would have suited him just fine, but Charles was having none of it. They had all of the Emerald Coast to go before Saint-Malo.

'It's fantastic, you'll see, and there'll be loads to tell Adèle about.'

An hour later, they were back on the road.

The drive from Saint-Brieuc to Saint-Malo was not part of the Tour route; it was more of an 'in-between' stage. But it was their favourite one so far. Once again, George and Charles regretted not being able to stay longer, in spite of the wind and the threatening clouds. Here, unlike anywhere else, the visitors were enchanted by the bad weather. It revealed the mysterious nature of the region, its capricious character. It revealed the strength of Brittany's spirit.

By the time the two adventurers arrived in Erquy, forty kilometres from Saint-Brieuc, George had already sent two texts to Adèle.

They walked along the beaches at Cap d'Erquy at high tide, passing the windswept dunes with the grey moor beyond them. They had put on their fleeces and jackets, and clutched their caps with every fresh gust of wind. The sound of the waves, the smell of iodine, the sand, the fleeting clouds, the cries of children darting about around their parents – it all seemed to dance in a vivid whirlwind, all seemed so alive. They felt as though the swirling, exotic air was purifying their lungs. Nevertheless it was bitterly cold and after a while the companions sought refuge in a restaurant that looked out onto the beach.

Once they had sat down, Charles, who was still rubbing his hands to warm them up, pointed to the beach.

'Look at that madman down there. He must be off his rocker!'

George looked in the direction Charles was pointing, where a man dressed in nothing but a pair of swimming trunks was marching towards the sea with determination.

'No! He won't do it!' said George.

'And he's no spring chicken either. I'll bet you he's in his sixties at least. No, he's not going to … And he's done it! In one go as well!'

The man had dived into the waves.

'Bloody hell, he's got a death wish!' exclaimed George. 'That'll finish him off. Where are the lifeguards? We should do something!'

The waiter, who had come to their table, cut in:

'Oh, don't worry about him, he does this every day. Come rain, wind or snow, he's out there. We're all used to it.'

'Even in the middle of winter?' asked Charles.

'Even in the middle of winter. Once my colleague saw him out there when it was minus five! I wasn't there, I take my holiday in February. But my colleague saw him. Minus five it was outside!'

George and Charles stared at him, their mouths open in shock.

'But we don't mind him too much. It's a real spectacle for customers, I can tell you that much! They love it! Right, what can I bring you? Some scallops perhaps?'

'Oh, go on then,' said Charles. 'If we don't eat scallops in Erquy, where will we eat them, right?'

'And you won't be the only ones, as you're about to find out. It's Saturday, and the old chap swimming down there is going to come up here. Every Saturday he treats himself to a seafood feast. You'll see.'

And indeed, after about five minutes (the feat was carefully timed by Charles), the man picked up the large towel that he had left by the water, walked up the beach, his back straight as a rod, and disappeared from sight. Less than ten minutes later he walked into the restaurant. George and Charles recognised him by his wet hair under his cap, which he took off once he was inside; he was now very elegantly dressed in a bottle-green roll-neck and beige suit. He made his way to the table that had clearly been reserved for him, near where George and Charles were sitting. Charles couldn't resist saying something to this oddball.

'I say, you've got to be pretty robust to do what you just did.'

'Not at all, old chap,' the man replied, shaking out his napkin. 'You don't have to be robust, you have to be a Breton!'

George wondered how many times the waiters had heard this line. Charles didn't pursue the conversation; his interlocutor seemed like someone who wanted to be left in peace.

Over lunch, Charles and George went over the practical details of the next stage of the Tour: hotels, timings, things to see, logistics ... Then they reminisced about what they had seen over the past few days. All of this was peppered with anecdotes from the Tour, along with a few that were completely unrelated. As their dessert was being served, it was now the man-fish who addressed them.

'Excuse me, sorry to interrupt, but ... are you doing a tour of Brittany?'

'No, good sir,' answered Charles proudly. 'Better than that, we're doing the Tour de France!'

'Good grief!'

'We're doing it in a car, not on bikes, mind you.'

'Good grief even so! May I ask which route you're taking?'

Charles and George explained their itinerary to him, with a brief description of what they had already seen. Their neighbour was impressed.

'My word, I would have loved the chance to do that.'

'Well, what's stopping you? It's obviously not your health.'

'Actually that's exactly what's stopping me. Because if I didn't have my daily dip, who knows what I'd catch. You never know at seventy-six.'

'You're seventy-six?' exclaimed Charles. 'I've got to say, you certainly don't look it. I'd like to say "like me", but to be honest, you put me to shame.'

'And you really swim every day?' asked George.

'Every day. For the last twenty years.'

'And when you're away? That must have happened once or twice.'

'Ah, you mean the times in life when I've had to stray far from my home country – by which I mean Brittany, of course. Well, if I wasn't close to the Channel, the Atlantic, or the Mediterranean – although the Mediterranean—'

'Oh, the Mediterranean isn't really the sea,' George cut in, 'more like a huge bath tub, really.'

'Ah yes, I agree with you there. Anyway, if I can't swim, then it's an hour of walking first thing. But not an hour of pottering around, mind, a proper walk! Standing up straight, head held high.'

'Well then, the Tour de France would be perfect for you! Because we've done some good walks, I can tell you!'

'You're not wrong there,' replied George a little wearily, whose knees had started to ache just thinking about it.

The three pensioners moved their tables together and ordered coffees – and a green tea for Charles. The swimmer's name was Marcel. He was a retired army officer who lived in Erquy with his wife Jacqueline, five years his junior. Every Saturday she went to a water aerobics class at the gym, and he took the opportunity to treat himself to seafood.

'I think we'd get on well, the three of us,' Marcel declared. 'Hats off to you both, you've chosen life! Down with the dictatorship of aches and pains, and down with doctors who stuff us with pills, and down with the daily routine that's sending us to our graves. We've got to *rebel*. And when the end comes, well, we can bow out with dignity.'

'Ah!' George cried, but didn't finish his sentence and carried on playing with the breadcrumbs on the table.

'See, I've got a plan,' Marcel continued. 'The day I'm no longer able to go swimming, I'm just going to go anyway. I'll drag myself to the sea and I'll swim until they lose sight of me. And that'll be it. And I've told my wife, I said to her: "When that day comes, Jacqueline, if I catch you trying to fish me out of the water ..."'

After several heavy sighs, George murmured:

'That's precisely why I'm doing this Tour ... It's the last chance ...'

His words had woken Charles out of his daydream but Marcel interrupted him.

'Once again, gentlemen, I congratulate you! Ah, how I'd love to come with you ...'

When their bills came, Marcel offered them a last drink on him. As it had with Ginette, the brandy made George feel as though he'd drunk from the fountain of youth. He got up and made an announcement:

'Well, my friends, the time has come to see if I've got any Breton blood in me.'

Charles and Marcel stared at him uncomprehendingly.

'I'll be back in ten minutes.'

Marcel started to laugh. Then the penny dropped for Charles.

'What? You're not saying you're going to swim ...'

'Oh no, just my feet,' George corrected him. 'I'm a beginner. And anyway, I don't have a towel!'

'I can lend you mine, George!' said Marcel enthusiastically. 'I dare say we're on first-name terms by now, aren't we?'

George brushed off the offer of a towel, and headed in the direction of the beach. He came back a minute later to get his mobile phone, which he had left on the table, then set off again, seaward-bound.

Charles and Marcel watched him walking into the distance. He had taken off his shoes and socks and pulled his trousers up to his knees, revealing his meagre calves that seemed hesitant to approach the waves.

Charles turned to Marcel with a look of concern.

'Are you sure he's not going to catch pneumonia, or hypothermia, or God knows what else?'

'Well, I've always said that seawater works wonders for me, but that doesn't mean it works for everyone.'

This was not the answer Charles had been hoping for.

George felt the cold, wet sand under his white feet. This was not a good start. He had imagined something more silky, and more importantly, something warmer. He knew that the other two were watching him and he couldn't back out now. He was starting to regret his earlier bravado. That had been the brandy's fault. He took a step forwards as the tide was ebbing and gingerly placed his foot in the sand that was soaked in icy water; but the tide was already rushing back and rising above his ankles. Damn it was cold. So cold that he could feel a sharp pain all the way up to his knees. It was unbearable, but he didn't want to give up now. He walked along the beach just above the shoreline, to get used to the cold. Then he let the water lap over his toes and bit by bit advanced into the water, until finally, about fifty metres down the beach, he had water around his ankles again, this time with considerably less discomfort.

He had completely forgotten about his companions and their raspberry brandy back on the seafront. He was simply enjoying the eccentricity, the audacity even, of walking barefoot in the sea on a cold day in October. The audacity of it! It had been years since he'd done something daring. The water, which had been glacial, then chilly, now felt refreshing. He felt a strange sense of physical well-being, as though his body had been purified or rejuvenated. George's thoughts turned to his only daughter. He would have liked to share this moment with her. She might have been proud of him, as he felt proud of himself now. It would have made her smile. No, actually, she would almost certainly have started worrying about him. The Françoise he knew today would have told him to get out of the water. The Françoise he remembered from twenty years ago would have laughed with him, would have told him he was mad, secretly wanting to join in the fun. He missed her. It was ironic, really: he had been so careful to keep her in the dark, and now he wished she were here to see it all with him.

For fifty years, George had been married to a woman he had loved and respected. He knew better than anyone that life was better when shared with someone else. But since Arlette's death, there hadn't been much worth sharing. Cups of tea with Charles, a cheque in the post for family birthdays, and that was about it. Time had passed; he had grown old and fallen out of step. Out of step with the world, with youth, with his grass and his tomato plants. He had ended up alone, left behind by the peloton, and had resigned himself to thinking that maybe this was not such a bad thing, that he preferred to be left the hell alone. And now here he was, his feet in the Channel (or was it the Atlantic? He wasn't sure and didn't dare ask anyone), realising that perhaps being left alone wasn't always better. That maybe he didn't even want to be left alone at all.

George continued his walk along the beach. He looked around and saw that Marcel and Charles had become small dots; they were still sitting together. He felt good walking through the water, listening to the sounds of crashing waves and birdcalls. The voices in his head were more excited than ever. They were whispering to him that he should call Ginette. That was what mobile phones were for, weren't they? So you could call people from totally unlikely places like a beach in Erquy. Or if a phone call was a bit too impulsive, what about a little text message?

George protested inwardly. It was ridiculous to be tapping away on a little machine like a madman when he could be appreciating the wild beauty of his surroundings, the nature all around him and the windswept dunes. It was enough to make a poet of him. And would Lord Byron, in thrall to the vivid spring colours of Nottinghamshire, have spent his time there sending text messages like there was no tomorrow? Of course not. But the Romantic poet had praised nature in all its glory in his heartfelt and lengthy correspondence. So if text messages had been around in his day, George felt sure he would have been glued to his phone as well. And anyway, this time he had something to say to Ginette.

Grey sky @ Erquy, wtr is nice, we r both doin well. We r lookin 4wrd 2 cing u in Nantes. Best, George.

(Grey sky at Erquy, water is nice, we are both doing well. We are looking forward to seeing you in Nantes. Best, George.)

He also saw he had received two replies from Adèle, telling him what she was doing and envying him his travels. Little Adèle. He gazed into the horizon for a few moments, took a deep breath of fresh air and stood in the water, not moving for some time.

Charles and Marcel watched him from the restaurant, without saying a word.

It was not for want of things to talk about. The conversation had been kept up for some time, and had been all the more animated because Marcel and Charles kept finding things in common. First, Marcel had declared that his daily dip had kept him in such good shape that it ought to have been funded by the health service. He couldn't have picked a better topic to win Charles over.

'I completely agree!' exclaimed Charles. 'I completely agree! And I'll tell you something, Marcel, that's not the only thing we should be able to get on the health service ... There's also ... *playing cards!* We have a *belote* championship, once a month, you know. Not that everyone is obsessed with card games back home – it's Chanteloup, not Las Vegas. But even so, firstly, loads of people do it. And second, you should see everyone arriving at two o'clock, when it starts. There are folks in wheelchairs, people who've lost their legs, who've got problems with their ulcers, their kidneys and all sorts. Some have even had chemo, and that's not the last of it, you know what I mean? But after the first round everyone's stopped complaining! By the time it gets to five o'clock, we're all breathless! Some of us would start dancing on the tables if we could!'

Charles banged the table for emphasis. Marcel was nodding in agreement.

'I'm not much of a cards person myself,' he said. 'But I see what you're saying. My sister, for example, lives in Reugny, in the Touraine, near Vouvray. Now, every year, around the end of October – it'll be happening soon, now I come to think of it – they hold a *bernache* festival. Do you know what *bernache* is?'

'No, but I'd like to find out. We'll be driving through the Touraine before long.'

'OK, well, *bernache* is somewhere between grape juice and wine. Actually, the more of it you drink, the more you become sure that it's closer to wine than juice. But anyway, I still think … I still think *bernache*, Charles, should be provided by the health service as well!'

'Well of course, if it's somewhere between grape juice and wine, and more wine than juice, what's not to like?'

'Anyway, so my sister,' Marcel continued, 'she organises the festival, and there's a fair and a junk sale as well. She does all that with the local pensioners' club and all the oldies in the area love it, it's just like you were saying. They're suddenly full of get-up-and-go. If you ask me, it was *bernache* that Jesus used to raise the dead!'

Marcel and Charles burst out laughing, slapping the table and clutching their stomachs. They were a picture of good fun.

'Ah,' said Charles playfully, 'there's something else that the health service should cover: gardening.'

'Hmm,' said Marcel, doubtfully. 'I tend to think that gardening gives one a bad back, actually.'

'Bad back, my foot!' said Charles indignantly. 'If you've got a bad back, that's because you don't keep your garden properly! A lovely big vegetable patch with pretty flowers for the missus to put in her vases for when the guests come, what could be better for your spirits than that? And what do you say to fishing?'

'Oh, fishing,' conceded Marcel. 'Well, I won't disagree with you there. That should be covered too, especially if the weather's good, April–May time, and you're going out with your radio.'

'You take a radio with you? That's not the way to do it! I like a bit of calm, myself. There's always such a racket at home, when we've got the whole brood there ... But if you want my opinion, you'd catch more fish without the radio.'

'Come off it! The fish in Brittany love hearing the ten o'clock news.'

'And what about the Tour de France?' cried Charles. 'Covered or not?'

They looked at each other without speaking, their eyes shining with their new-found affinity.

'Not covered, Charles. *Sponsored!* By the government itself!'

The two men started laughing again. Then the laughter dissipated and they gradually fell silent, their gaze naturally drifting towards the sea. They could see George in the distance, standing in the water. He seemed to be peering closely at something in his hand. Charles was used to this by now; he knew that the object in question was George's mobile phone.

After a long silence, his eyes still fixed on the beach, Charles murmured:

'Another thing that the health service should cover, Marcel, is George's granddaughter's text messages.'

When George got back to the restaurant, his cheeks rosy, his feet tingling, and his spirits high, they paid the bill and collected their things. As he was pulling on his jacket, Marcel asked his two new friends:

'If you're heading to Saint-Malo this evening, will you be passing through Dinard?'

'Yes, we should do,' answered Charles.

'Would you like to have dinner with me there? I know a wonderful restaurant. Well, I'll have to call my wife to warn her, but otherwise I'm free. And I can show you the pink granite coast and all that along the way. And you can't leave here without seeing the port, of course.'

George and Charles were all for it, especially Charles, who never liked saying goodbye.

As arranged, they followed Marcel's Citroën C4 in the Scenic. They stopped in the centre of Erquy and Charles and George got to see why it was called 'the red resort'. They walked from the Port des Hôpitaux to the beach at Saint-Pabu; the beautiful and varied surroundings inspired another text message to Adèle:

Anothr place 2 note 4 wen u come 2 Brttany: here, beaches 4 relaxin nd hiking trails. We r wiv a nu frnd, Marcel, the 1 who goes swimmin evry day. We r eatin wiv him in Dinard this eve.

(Another place to note for when you come to Brittany: here, beaches for relaxing and hiking trails. We are here with a new friend, Marcel, the one who goes swimming every day. We are eating with him in Dinard this evening.)

Marcel also gave them a brief explanation of the local birdlife. He explained that the birds here predicted the weather and guided the fishermen. He pointed out various different species: terns, seagulls, cormorants, kittiwakes, guillemots and gannets. George was fascinated. This was much more interesting than a museum.

They stopped off at Cap Fréhel, la Frenaye Bay and Saint-Cast-le-Guildo, the peninsula with seven stunning beaches. They saw the Pointe de la Garde and the seawall that ran along the impressive beach, and admired the view of the Ebihens archipelago and the Saint-Jacut peninsula. Marcel told them they must try Saint-Cast spider crab – but that would have to be for another day. They finally got to Dinard at around six o'clock.

Marcel gave them the grand tour of the town. Charles and George discovered the faded charm of the elegant seaside resort, with its seafront villas. Dinard may have displayed traces of the splendour of its prosperous past, but it clearly also attracted a young, fashionable crowd judging by the sports cars they kept spotting. They ate in a magnificent belle époque restaurant, where the plants either side of the entrance matched the vivid colours of the mural mosaics. Although initially George and Charles did not feel quite at ease in this setting, by the end of the evening it was as though they were in their own dining room, thanks to the good food, the good company, and the affable owner who came over to welcome them.

They parted as firm friends, promising to meet again soon. Charles and George did not get to their hotel in Saint-Malo until late, and went to bed almost immediately. As he was reading Adèle's most recent text, George suddenly remembered he had forgotten to buy the Agatha Christie book, and tomorrow was a Sunday. Never mind, he'd buy it in Nantes. Nantes, where he'd be seeing Ginette again. He thought of the text he'd sent, and felt like an awkward teenager. He grimaced and buried his face in the pillow. He was definitely too old for all of this.

Sunday 5 October

Saint-Malo–Forêt de Paimpont (Ille-et-Vilaine)

George had just one regret, and that was that it wasn't 16 October. An extremely high tide had been predicted for Saint-Malo that day, and it promised to be a spectacular event: a firework display of spray and water crashing against the rocks and flying into the air. At low tide the rock pools and sand banks were uncovered; this was the kingdom of the crabs usually concealed by the sea. He explained about the tides to Adèle in a text, and then to Charles as they walked along the seafront.

Even on an average day, the town was well worth a visit. The rows of pointy-roofed houses, the restless sea, the stormy sky, the bending trees sculpted by the wind: Saint-Malo was painted in every single shade of grey. This was where the Atlantic met the Channel; Charles would have put money on it not being a happy encounter.

They chose to walk along the sea wall rather than venture inside the ramparts to the old town. They ate lunch in the wide harbour and watched fishing boats, cargo ships and battleships endlessly coming and going.

Afterwards, they got back on the road and arrived at the forest of Paimpont just before 4 p.m. Charles was eager to visit the Louison Bobet Museum before it closed, but George had a different plan in mind: he wanted to see the mythical Brocéliande Forest. This put Charles's back up: it was all very well, the Arthurian legend, the romantic woodland, the druids and all the rest of it, but they really were moving at a snail's pace and now he was going to miss the Louison Bobet Museum.

In the end, George said that if he was going to be like that, they ought to go their separate ways. He would drive – just this once – and drop Charles off at his museum, then go and admire the *real* hidden treasures of the region. Charles agreed and not another word was exchanged until they parted ways at Saint-Méen-le-Grand, in front of the famous cycling museum. Two hours later they met back at the same place. George got into the passenger seat and with remarkable stubbornness, both continued to sulk. They went to bed without having dinner; neither of them wanted to eat together, yet neither wanted to deprive the other of the car. They each went to bed not knowing what the other had done for two hours, when in fact they had done exactly the same thing.

Monday 6 October

Forêt de Paimpont (Ille-et-Vilaine)-Nantes (Loire-Atlantique)

Charles went down to breakfast; his joints ached, his back hurt and he had had a terrible night's sleep. The mattress had been awful, he was going to say something to the receptionist – except that they were leaving that morning and actually there wasn't much point. When he got to the ground floor he was distracted from his train of thought by the melodious sounds of a shouting match. It didn't take him long to make out George's voice.

'Seriously,' George berated the receptionist, 'if we're not paying for a good bed, what the heck are we paying for? Tell me, what are those forty-seven euros for exactly, the paintings on the walls? Because I don't know if you've noticed, but it's not exactly the Louvre here! Or are we paying for the sound of the little birdies? Because I don't mind telling you they were drowned out by the toilet flush – I'd have thought there were better things to listen to in the countryside! I didn't use the TV, your breakfast is only good enough for sparrows, so would you please be good enough to have my mattress changed, pronto. Has the thing been changed since the war? The first or the second?'

'I'm sorry, Monsieur, it's just ... the credit crunch—'

'Oh, that's a good one, that is! I knew the financial crisis was keeping people up at night but this is taking the joke a bit far! Madame, the credit crunch, the credit crunch!' he said, waving his arms around melodramatically. 'And what sort of crisis is going on here, if I may be so bold? It's a crisis of common sense, that's what! And don't try and tell me this hasn't been going on for years. So before I have a crisis of my own, I'd advise you to get a wriggle on and get me a first-class replacement! With springs and goose down and all the rest of it! And preferably before Christmas! Thank you, and good day!'

George turned on his heel and almost collided with Charles, who took him by the arm and whispered to him:

'But George, we're leaving this morning, what do you care whether they change your mattress or not?'

'Oh no, I'm catching up on the sleep I missed; I'm going to take a siesta this afternoon and that's final! We'll leave when we leave. I'm going back to bed as soon as this young lady finds me something that actually resembles one!'

George marched into the breakfast room and helped himself to an enormous, overflowing bowl of cornflakes. It was the first time Charles had seen George eat cereal, but it occurred to him that there were times in life when you just wanted a big bowl of whatever you could get, and this was one of those moments.

Neither of them spoke during breakfast. George grumbled

something and, almost instinctively, reached for his phone in his jacket pocket. He rapidly typed a message and sent it with a brisk click. It was tacitly understood that they would drive to Nantes as soon as George had caught up on his missed sleep. They'd drive through the night if they had to.

At last the receptionist came up to George and offered him complimentary use of the best room in the hotel until the end of the day, or even until the next morning if he wanted. The offer was duly and gracefully accepted. George tried the bed and couldn't help grinning. It was sublime. Charles took the opportunity to remind him that he hadn't got any shut-eye either, so they both lay down in the king-size bed. George demonstrated just how seriously he was taking the nap by putting on his striped pyjamas and placing his slippers next to the bed. He fell asleep as soon as he'd sent Adèle a text.

He was woken up by the sound of his telephone ringing. He picked up before he remembered where he was or what time it was.

'Hello, George? It's Ginette here,' she said cheerfully.

'Oh, Ginette.'

'Are you OK?'

'Yes.'

'I'm not disturbing you, am I?'

'Err … no.'

'OK, good, I just wanted to arrange where to meet tomorrow.'

'Oh yes.'

'How about half past twelve at your hotel? Would that be alright?'

'Yes, yes.'

'Good. And you're still planning to stay at the Hôtel de France, aren't you?'

'Yes.'

'OK, so twelve-thirty then,' said Ginette.

'Yes.'

'See you tomorrow then,' she said, sounding much less perky now.

'See you tomorrow, uh, Ginette.'

George was now completely awake, and utterly confused. It was dark in the bedroom. Had he really been asleep for that long? Charles was lying in the darkness beside him. He checked the time on his phone: 18:47. He turned on the bedside lamp and woke Charles. The two men were startled by how long they had slept, but they were also starving; they hadn't eaten anything since the previous evening apart from the frugal hotel breakfast. They had missed two meals in two days; they had to make up for it. They wolfed down their dinner in silence before setting off again in the car. It occurred to George that they hadn't really made it up since the incident with the Bobet Museum and the forest of Brocéliande. Not a good sign.

They arrived at the hotel just before midnight and went up to their rooms without a word. George unpacked, put on his pyjamas and slid under the covers straight away. But, of course, it was impossible to fall asleep. Luckily Adèle was shooting all night and he had a whole list of things to tell her – all about Dinard, Brocéliande, the spat with the receptionist, the spat with Charles. Except that he probably wouldn't mention the fight with Charles, as he wasn't exactly proud of his behaviour. Even so, he and his granddaughter were up half the night texting each other. One text in particular warmed the old man's heart:

Adèle 07/10/2008 03:14
Nite shoot difficult + lonely, so thx grndpa 4 spnding eve wiv me!
(Night shoot difficult and lonely, so thanks Grandpa for spending the evening with me!)

He lay there looking at the message long after they'd said goodnight.

Tuesday 7 October

Nantes (Loire-Atlantique)

George got up very late; Charles hadn't come to get him. He was clearly still sulking, which actually suited George just fine; it had allowed him to make up for the almost sleepless night and given him plenty of time to prepare for his date with Ginette. Ah, he had forgotten to tell Charles that his sister was arriving at lunchtime. Damn. It was almost eleven. He called reception.

'Good morning, I'd like to leave a message for Monsieur Charles Lepensier, please.'

'Yes, of course. If you'd just like to hold on, I'll put you through to his room,' said a polite female voice.

'No, no!' he said hastily. 'I don't want to disturb him. I just want to leave a message.'

'Very good, Monsieur.'

'OK, could you please tell him that Monsieur George Nicoleau says Ginette will be at the hotel at half past twelve?'

'Of course, I'll pass on the message.'

'Thank you, Madame, goodbye.'

By five past twelve he was showered, shaved, and dressed, had put on cologne, dusted off his cap, cleaned his glasses and shined his shoes. In short, he was ready to go, but he still had almost half an hour to wait. He sat down on the bed and thought about turning on the television but it wouldn't have been like at home, with this complicated TV set and all these channels he didn't know.

Home ... His little house in Chanteloup suddenly seemed very far away. He started thinking about all the reasons he had decided to do the Tour; they now all seemed rather dubious. But he brushed these thoughts from his mind: he'd have plenty of time to worry about all that later. For the moment he had to concentrate on waiting for Ginette.

At half past twelve he was sitting at a table in the hotel restaurant, fiddling with the corners of his napkin. He had been caught off guard when the waiter had asked, 'And how many will you be?' He had told himself it was probably best to get a table for three, even if he was hoping that Charles wouldn't come. Not that he was sick of his company; they hadn't fallen out that badly. But he would have immediately picked up on George's nervousness, and that bothered George. Because he *was* nervous; he felt as though it was the first time he'd done something like this. Perhaps one never stopped getting butterflies on these occasions. Or perhaps he was just a little rusty when it came to matters of the heart; after all, he hadn't been on a date for about sixty years.

Ginette arrived at twelve thirty-two. George thought she looked even lovelier than the last time he had seen her. He couldn't put his finger on what had changed – perhaps it was her make-up, or her hair – but whatever it was, it had worked. She was wearing a pale pink blouse, an elegant pearl necklace and a red wool jacket with a rather modern cut, which showed her lightly tanned skin to its best advantage. They greeted each other. George, ever the gentleman, pulled out her chair for her. He tried to explain Charles's absence with the story of the bad mattress, the Louison Bobet Museum, the message that he'd left at reception and all the rest of it, but the more he talked, the more the whole thing was sounding like an elaborate ploy to be alone with her; he got so tangled up in it that finally Ginette cut him off.

'Yes, I understand. Well, never mind, I'm sure we'll see him this afternoon.'

For once, George had no complaints about the meal. In fact, he was totally oblivious to everything: the drinks, the food, the other diners, whom he would doubtless otherwise have found pretentious, even the dubious modern art on the walls and the overloaded dessert trolley. He only had eyes for Ginette. And for himself; he was far more self-conscious than usual and he was not enjoying it. When the dessert course came around, he went quiet and stopped listening to Ginette, who was talking rather a lot. Not because he wasn't interested in what she had to say, but because he needed to concentrate very carefully on the manoeuvre he was about to carry out. This was not at all like riding a bike. He finally plucked up the courage to take Ginette's hand in his. Ginette stopped talking for a moment, then carried on almost immediately, a little quicker this time. But she left her hand in George's.

After dessert, the conversation took a decidedly different turn. Without a doubt, George's gesture and Ginette's acceptance had radically altered the tone. Now they could, if they wanted to, talk about making plans together, as long as they remained appropriate. This was an extremely delicate phase: if said plans became too ambitious, they risked taking things too fast; on the other hand, no discussion of any plans at all might have implied that neither of them was taking this seriously. George felt about as relaxed as an amateur tightrope walker with rheumatism. Luckily, Ginette found the happy medium. She began by admitting that her social diary was packed full over the next few weeks; between friends that she had invited to stay with her and their reciprocal offers, she barely had a moment to herself. Nevertheless there was a small window in the whirlwind of her social arrangements where she would be at home alone for a week. And it wouldn't be too cold there yet, seeing as it was in fact the week after next. She was hoping to enjoy, she said to George, long walks along the beach and in the pine forests. Unfortunately, George was so nervous that he missed all the hints. It took a few more allusions, each less subtle than the previous one, before he understood – or rather, before he was sure he had not *mis*understood – that she was inviting him to Notre-Dame-de-Monts for the week after next.

It was all he could have hoped for. George felt satisfied with his tour of Brittany. All he wanted to do now was settle down in a comfortable place to enjoy his remaining years and send texts to his granddaughter. If this place also had Ginette in it, the offer became absolutely irresistible.

George and Ginette spent the afternoon wandering through the streets of Nantes; Ginette very much enjoyed the chance to play tour guide. She showed him the cathedral and the winding little side streets around it. They passed the Musée des Beaux-Arts, but George warned her that he was not a great lover of museums. As an alternative, he suggested going to look at the courthouse, as he had seen a photo of it in one of the magazines in his hotel room. They took a taxi and arrived in front of a huge contemporary structure made of black metal, concrete and glass, which George, contrary to all expectation, was extremely impressed by; Ginette had assumed that his taste in architecture was rather more traditional. True to form, however, George still complained that in some places the detailing was a little sloppy. They spent a long time exploring the building, and George seized the chance to demonstrate his knowledge of construction and engineering. Ginette listened attentively. From the top of the courthouse, they were granted an incomparable view of Nantes and the Loire, which gushed beneath them in mud-coloured cascades.

In the late afternoon they called the hotel from George's mobile to find out if Charles had returned, but without success. They found a small gourmet restaurant just off Avenue Saint-André, a wide boulevard lined with elegant, understated buildings in the classical style. They enjoyed delicious food in a cosy atmosphere, and it was over a devilishly tasty chocolate fondant that their first day of romance came to a close.

*

George sat down on the edge of the bed surrounded by the imposing contemporary décor in the large, overpriced room. It was dark outside. He had sent his evening text to Adèle, but this time had not gone into too much detail about his day. He felt exhausted after all his adventures. Ginette had gone back to Notre-Dame-de-Monts, about an hour away from Nantes. At least this bed was comfortable. He had been seriously missing his home comforts since the beginning of the Tour. The room in Auray had been perfectly pleasant, and the one in Paimpont had been tolerable, in the end. The bedroom at Ginette's had been the most comfortable, and the breakfast there had been lively and convivial. Nevertheless, this epic journey was pretty tiring. He still hadn't quite recovered from the night at Paimpont and his body felt weary, although his spirits were high. He was worn out. Ginette's invitation couldn't have come at a better time.

George spent the evening sitting up in bed, going over the events of the day in his mind. How could he have forgotten all of his reasons for doing the Tour? He had spent so long devising this plan; the package wrapped in brown paper lying under his spare socks reminded him of all those reasons every time he packed and unpacked his bags. He had wanted to do the Tour to escape the agonisingly slow passing of time, to hurry destiny along. To be done with it all.

But that had been before. Before Ginette, before Adèle, before Brittany and its unexpected treasures, before his picnics with Charles, before he'd had a chance to discover that he still had some life left in him. Before. Before all of this he had thought his tank was empty. But now he knew there were still a few drops left to use. Perhaps even more than just a few drops. So why not share them? Calmly, unhurriedly. There was no rush, after all.

And so it was that George decided to end his Tour de France there. It was a surrender that ought to have been announced as a triumph.

Wednesday 8 October

Nantes (Loire-Atlantique)-Cholet (Maine-et-Loire)

George was relieved to see Charles in the breakfast room; he had been beginning to worry. Charles told him with a little smile that he had received the message, but had thought it might be better to give them some time alone. George returned his smile. No need to go into detail.

But the words that George had been going through in his head all night weren't coming out. What was more, he didn't want Charles to think that it was because of the ridiculous squabble by the Louison Bobet. He had to play this very carefully.

'Erm, Charles, I've got something to tell you. I think I might stop here, you know.'

'I see,' said Charles, suddenly sitting very straight in his seat.

'Yes. It's all very well going on an adventure, but it's hard on my old bones. I feel like such an old fool, and I'm sorry to have to let you down like this but sometimes you just have to listen to yourself and I can't keep going if my heart's not in it. Well, I say that; it's actually the rest of my body that needs a break. I've been thinking about it for the last few stages. I can't keep up any more.'

Charles said nothing.

'And I'll tell you something else, Charles. I didn't see any of Brocéliande Forest. Instead, I had a two-hour snooze in a supermarket car park in Saint-Méen. And it wasn't even a good nap, because we were cross with one another.'

'Funny you should say that,' Charles replied sadly. 'I didn't see any of the museum either; it was shut. So I had a little kip too, in the Café des Sports in Saint-Méen. And you're right, it's hard to sleep when you've … Well, you know what I mean.'

Charles looked more emotional than George had imagined, which threw him off guard. Almost in a whisper, Charles murmured:

'It's Ginette, isn't it?'

'Not just her … I mean, she is partly why,' George answered after a moment's hesitation. 'She's invited me to stay in Notre-Dame-de-Monts. To spend the week there. It'd be a good chance to recover after so many days on the road. And bloody good days they were too, by the way. That's why I think there's no shame in taking a little break.'

As if he hadn't heard any of this explanation, Charles looked at him with tears in his eyes, and asked in a quiet voice:

'Isn't there any way you could spend a week there after the last stage? Or we could even go before, if we could just go a little way further?'

It was the first time that George had seen Charles's vulnerable side, good old Charles with his rough farmers' hands, and it upset him a great deal. He felt as though Charles was hiding something from him. For the first time in years, he couldn't read his neighbour, and he was momentarily lost for words.

'Charles, it's not as if we're after the yellow jersey, right?'

The words he had repeated to himself over and over in his head now rang false.

Charles stared wordlessly down at his breakfast. After a long silence, he said:

'Ginette doesn't know what's going on. If she did, she'd never have invited you to stay with her.'

George was taken aback.

'W-what do you mean?' he stuttered. 'I've never kept anything from Ginette, I've never kept anything from anyone, I'm—'

'What I mean is, she doesn't know why I'm doing this.'

'Oh, Charles, you're doing it because it was your boyhood dream and we're all allowed to try and realise our boyhood dreams at the grand old age of eighty, there's no shame in that, none at all! And we've been gallivanting around like a couple of young boys for the last two weeks, but I'm sorry to say that my legs can't take any more and I wouldn't say no to a little break ... And who knows, maybe we'll even finish it some day.'

'No George,' Charles interrupted. 'That's not why I'm here. Of course I've been dreaming of this for yonks but whether it was this or something else, it's not a lack of anything else to do that's the problem. I'm doing it because I need ...'

He paused for a moment, and then continued:

'I need you and this Tour and to get out and see the world

because my mind is getting worse by the day, George. It's the curse of old age; my brain is *degenerating* and it doesn't matter how many times they tell you that that's just the way it is, and there's no avoiding it, believe me George, when it does hit you it's a living nightmare. And there's no medication for it, there's nothing but the loony bin and big black holes in your memory. So the only thing the doctors tell you is that you've got to keep your noggin working at all costs. And how? They tell you to do crosswords, that's what they tell old fogeys like us, because they think that's all we're good for. But I'm telling you, you need crosswords and wordsearches and anagrams and Sudokus and all the rest of it just to keep your head straight; you need more puzzles than *Téléstar* can print. And I've had it up to here with crosswords, I can't stand them any more. I know all there is to know, all the "ing"s and the "ed"s, the abbreviations of every country; I could do crosswords for France. OK, then there's *belote*, and gardening, and letter-writing, and Scrabble – if you listened to them you'd be doing bloody basket weaving before long. But I've had enough of all that, George, I can't do it any more ... There's something eating away at my brain, and it's destroying everything: my memories, familiar faces, even the rooms in my home and the names of my grandkids. I've forgotten all the things I know. All of my memories have a chunk missing from them, and sometimes I get terrified that one day everything will just go, bam, and then what will be left of me? I'll be all hollowed out like a shell on the beach, with nothing left, nothing – because what's the point of being old if you don't have any memories? Is life worth living when you've got no one left, because you've forgotten who your family are?

It's worth bugger all, George. Bugger all. There you go. The only thing Thérèse and I could come up with was this Tour de France. Changing scenery every day, seeing new things, meeting new people, learning … And at the same time I got to do what I'd always wanted, so when it was a choice between that and crosswords … We didn't really believe it at the start, because you weren't sure, so I didn't let myself get too involved. But now, now we're doing it. Maybe it won't make a difference, maybe the lights are going to go out anyway and there's nothing I can do about it. But maybe not, maybe it'll work. Thérèse believes in it. As for me, I'm not convinced yet, but what can I do? Even if it doesn't help, it's definitely not doing any harm. And you know what, maybe I do believe in it, even if it's just because I've got to believe in something. There you go. And Ginette doesn't know. She doesn't know that her brother's losing his marbles. If she did, she wouldn't have invited you to Notre-Dame-de-Monts.'

Charles stopped talking. George didn't know what to say. He felt a lump in his throat. Why hadn't he seen this earlier? He should have worked it out from the incident with the petrol pump, and from the leftovers after the picnic at Châteauneuf-du-Faou … And there had been other signs, now that he thought about it, like the day he forgot how to make a cup of tea. He now understood why Charles, who was normally unbeatable when it came to trivia, hadn't joined in the recounting of the Tour's historic moments.

What was he supposed to say? That the Tour was all very well, but what about when it was over? Was he going to go on a tour of the world? These days nothing was as far away as it had once been, it probably wouldn't even take him that long …

Was he planning on roaming the globe like a nomad until the end of his days, separating himself from his loved ones so he wouldn't forget them? Charles was right, there was a lot of talk of dementia and so on, but he didn't really know anything about it. It was something that happened to other people. And now he saw one of his friends clinging to illusions, trying to fight it. This Tour de France now seemed utterly absurd. At that moment he wished more than anything that he were one of life's optimists, he wished he could believe what his friend was telling him, believe that this was making him better, heck, he wished at that moment that he believed in God, because God was capable of miracles.

Charles broke the silence.

'I've got to tell you, George, I feel better for telling you. Keeping it a secret this whole time was ... Well, anyway I told you because you should know Ginette asked you without knowing all of this. But I guess if your joints are playing up, there's nothing we can do. Nothing we can do.'

It was a while before George had the courage to reply.

'Yes, there is.'

That same afternoon, they were heading towards stage five. And this time they were determined to see it through.

'And the Tour de France is off again! Over to you, Jean-Paul Brouchon, our man on the starting line!' said George exuberantly as he plugged in his seatbelt. The companions got back on the road with an enthusiasm neither of them had felt since the first day of the Tour – and even on that day there had been a lot less laughter. Charles's revelation had marked a new phase of their friendship. They could now say without hesitation that they were no longer *neighbours*, they were *friends*. Charles was visibly relieved to have shared his anxiety with George. He had also had a long telephone conversation with his sister. It had come as a shock to her, but she wholeheartedly agreed that some mental exercise was just what he needed. And George would not go to see her in Notre-Dame-de-Monts for the moment, but it was agreed he would come in November.

George was feeling so cheerful on the road from Nantes to Cholet that he started whistling *Y'a d'la joie*, the famous Charles Trenet song that reminded him of his childhood. Charles joined in, admittedly a little out of tune, but the end result was marvellous. And then all of a sudden, the words came pouring out of Charles's mouth: '*Miracle sans nom à la station Javel/ On voit le métro qui sort de son tunnel/ Grisé de soleil de chansons et de fleurs/ Il court vers le bois, il court à toute vapeur/ Y'a d'la joie bonjour bonjour les hirondelles!*'

He sang the song all the way through. The lyrics surged up from the distant past and seemed to fill him with a fresh burst of energy. Just before the last verse, Charles was hit in his excitement by a wave of false modesty and said:

'Oh, I don't think I can remember the rest.'

'Even so, I'm impressed!' said George. '"You did what you could, but you blew me away!"'

Charles thought for a few moments and then cried out:

'Brambilla! Pierre Brambilla! That's what he said to Jean Robic when he won the Tour in '47!'

'Correct!'

'So I haven't forgotten everything, then! Still got something between the ears!'

Slowly but surely, the Tour route was leading them back to their native region. They spent the night in Cholet with friends of Charles. After a challenging day Charles was able to relax with his friends, while George got an early night, claiming various aches and pains. In truth he was behind in his correspondence with Adèle; he caught up that evening with six texts updating her on the events of the last few days, from his day out in Nantes to the conversation with Charles. He mentioned Ginette, of course, without saying too much, but he knew Adèle would be able to read between the lines. And while he was about it, he sent a text to Ginette. Neither woman replied instantly and so, just this once, he switched off his phone, put in his earplugs and fell into a deep, untroubled sleep.

Thursday 9 October

Cholet (Maine-et-Loire)–La Celle-Guenand (Indre-et-Loire)

They took great joy in driving down the roads that passed through Bressuire, Mauléon, Les Herbiers and Thouars. These were the roads they had driven down all their lives; the names sounded familiar and comforting. They fitted in here. They knew what kind of bread they would find in the bakeries, they could name all the plants, trees, and even the weeds. They knew which newspapers would be on sale in the newsagents and saw familiar old men waiting to cross the road. They would doubtless recognise the names on the village war memorials, names of families who still lived nearby. George and Charles saw their little corner of the world with new eyes. They had been looking at the same things all their lives, but only now were they really paying attention.

They were so close to home that Charles and Thérèse had

arranged to meet. God knows how they managed to arrange it, thought George to himself, because Charles didn't have a mobile phone. Returning the favour that Charles had done him, George decided to give the couple some time alone and went to sit in a café in the centre of Thouars with a seven-euro menu. There were a few other pensioners sitting inside. With the customary cloth over his shoulder, the owner was talking to a local sitting at the bar. It was technically forbidden to smoke inside so he kept going back and forth to the entrance, filling the room with smoke as he went.

George instinctively reached for his phone to give him something to play with and pass the time. He had received several texts from Adèle and one from Ginette. Two little old men nursing Duralex tumblers called over to him:

'So young man, you're playing at mobile phones just like the kids, eh?'

'Well, I've got to,' George answered politely. 'For the granddaughter, you know how it is.'

And he turned his attention back to his text message, but the two men were clearly in a playful mood:

'No, I dunno how it is, and I dun' want to know. If we're meant to do everything the kids do these days just to bloody talk to 'em, I dunno … young people these days can't go a 'undred metres without tap-tap-tapping at their phones.'

And he imitated someone frantically writing a text. Before George had time to think to himself that this speech sounded familiar, the owner's wife rescued him by murmuring confidentially:

'Would you like to sit in the dining room upstairs? It's a little calmer up there.'

The dining room was pretty, with walls lined with tapestries. The owner's wife cleared the table and her iron, which she had left by the window, and gave him cutlery and a napkin.

Finally, he could concentrate on his texts. Ginette's was mainly about the weather. Adèle was unhappy with her working hours. Ginette had been to visit a friend in Les Sables-d'Olonne. Adèle was worried she was coming down with a cold. Ginette had decided to redecorate the kitchen before November. Adèle had recovered from the cold, thanks for asking. Nothing especially interesting, in short. Nothing urgent. How funny that it had taken him eighty-three years to see the enjoyment in small talk.

A little later, Charles came to meet George, told him Thérèse sent her love, and off they went again. They drove on to Le Grand-Pressigny, which had witnessed the Tour, and La Celle-Guenand, which had not but it did have a magnificent seventeenth-century château where they could stay for forty-five euros a night. Charles and George were struck by the vivid autumnal shades of the Touraine landscape, the pastel grey and orange of the fields, the slate roofs and delicate clouds that drifted across the sky like puffs of smoke, the lush green forests and the dried sunflowers that seemed to bow their brown heads in repentance. Any doubts George had felt about continuing the Tour had now vanished.

For as long as they could remember, there had been a tacit understanding that George was wealthier than Charles. And although this was a simple fact for George, Charles had never quite felt comfortable about the situation. So he was particularly proud to be taking George out for dinner that evening, in Le Petit-Pressigny. Not to just any restaurant either; this one was mentioned in all of the guidebooks, and had even been awarded the much-coveted Michelin star, with particular praise for its speciality: rustic bacon wrapped in buttered green cabbage, with black pudding and crackling. This was not Charles trying to show off to George, of course; rather the two companions had not had a chance to celebrate their epic undertaking properly, apart from the half-hearted Kir in Guémené. And so it was with genuine delight that George accepted the generous invitation. It was an evening to remember; the exquisite food and wine enhanced the euphoria of recent events. The pair were the last, and happiest, people in the restaurant. Neither of them wanted the day to end.

Friday 10 October

La Celle-Guenand–Loches (Indre-et-Loire)

When George pulled back the curtains in his bedroom in the château at La Celle-Guenand, he saw that the weather had cleared up again. It was cold, but there wasn't a cloud in the sky, and the newly gold leaves shone in the bright autumn sun. He had not slept well – the bed was very old, but this time he would not be complaining to reception. The chatelaine was lovely, an elegant and slim woman several years his senior. She looked after the château herself, renting out its dozen or so bedrooms to tourists, which must have been damn hard work. Everything looked worn out, threadbare and faded, yet George could tell that at one time his surroundings had been sumptuous. Even the carpet in his room had a noble history: the chatelaine had managed to acquire it through some well-connected friends during the renovation of the Ritz in Paris.

George was late for breakfast, which was served in the old armoury two floors down. The château had a magnificent staircase whose stone steps were worn from centuries of use. George was blinded for a moment by a ray of sunlight that came in through one of the large windows, causing him to lose his footing and slip just at the place where the steps were narrowest. The rest of his body tumbled after his feet, but how and in what order George would not be able to recall.

Fifty-eight minutes later he arrived at the hospital in Loches, where the doctor who saw him, although amused by the story of this unusual Tour de France, made it quite clear: the Tour ended here.

George was woken up by the arrival of his meal tray. After a moment of calm, the pain hit him with its full force. Was it the evening or the next day? No, it was evening. The nurse pushed his bed upright. He was weak, and felt as though his limbs were made of lead. He was finding it difficult to breathe. There was a drip attached to his arm and various machines were flashing next to him. He was alone, truly alone. He did not have his mobile phone next to him on the bedside table. There was a little sign stuck to the door: 'Mobile telephones strictly forbidden.' He didn't touch his meal. He took his various tablets, one of which he could see was a sleeping pill, reclined his bed again with the remote control and waited for the medication to take the pain away.

Sunday 12 October

Loches (Indre-et-Loire)

Adèle hung up the phone. Thérèse, the wife of George's Tour teammate Charles, had just told her that her grandfather was in hospital and that his condition was critical. It would be terrible for her career to miss several days of shooting; she might not even get a reference from the production company. She thought about it for a few moments until she realised that someone else could fetch the coffee and be responsible for all her other menial tasks for a few days. She was going to see her grandfather and that was that. The production manager was initially reluctant, until she saw that Adèle was not asking for permission so much as informing her of her decision, and so instead told her she had to be back as soon as possible. It would be difficult to find another runner at such short notice. For the first time, it occurred to Adèle that she was perhaps more useful to them than she thought.

If she travelled overnight both ways she would only have to miss one day of work. She would take the train to Paris on Monday evening, get a few hours' sleep on the sofa of a Parisian friend, then take an early train from the Gare Montparnasse, arriving in Tours in the morning, where she would take a regional train to Loches. She would arrive at the hospital by lunchtime. She would only have a few hours there: she would have to catch a train from Paris in the late afternoon. During this one visit she would have to be brave enough to tell her grandfather what she had been turning over and over in her mind since the previous evening. All she had to do was find the courage to say it aloud.

Of all the hardships that George now had to endure, one stood out from the rest: he was no longer able to send and receive texts. He didn't feel cut off from the world, but he did feel deprived of a great pleasure. He was unable to express himself, and he felt very far away from his granddaughter and from Ginette. As for the rest of it, the doctor had seen him this morning to inform him that he was in for a long day of tests, scans and examinations. He was going to be dragged from department to department all day long. He had to find a way of getting his phone back.

Just then, a hospital worker came in to collect his tray.

'Excuse me, Monsieur,' George asked, 'do you think you could pass me my jacket over there? I think my mobile is in one of the pockets.'

'Ah, I'm afraid mobile phones aren't allowed in the hospital building,' replied the man in his West African accent. 'And here they're real sticklers for it. Even the staff aren't allowed. But you can transfer your calls to your room telephone. Your family can call you on that.'

'Oh, but it's not the same thing.'

'I know, I hear you ... OK, well I'll have a look in your jacket anyway, where is it?'

'Oh thank you! It's there, in the left-hand pocket. Is it on?'

'No, it's off.'

'Oh.'

'I've got one too. My wife always says she doesn't know how anyone ever managed without them. And I always say: just fine!'

'Yes, exactly,' lied George.

'I had to get one when I was looking for work; at the job centre they told me it'd be much easier with a mobile. Oh, and of course, it's perfect for calling my mistress.'

George wasn't sure if he'd heard right. The man burst out laughing.

'I really had you there, didn't I!' and he let out another high-pitched laugh. 'You believed me, huh? Hehehehe! For calling my mistress, that's a good one!'

And actually, it had made the patient forget about all the machines and tubes for a few moments.

'Well, I don't want to keep you here all evening with my problems,' said George meekly.

'Oh no, I'm done for the night. But I like to talk with my patients now and again.'

George thought it was a little strange that he was talking about the patients as though they were his own. He felt rather ashamed when the man said:

'I was a doctor in Africa back in the day, well, a long time ago now …'

George thought to himself that it couldn't have been easy to be cleaning floors if you were a qualified doctor.

But the man continued:

'But I'm telling you, life's much better over here – especially with your thirty-five hour weeks!'

'And you're from Loches?' An African family would definitely have been something of a rarity in this area.

'No, Chaumussay. We have a little house in Chaumussay, it's a lovely place. Goes without saying that we're the only black people in the village, but everyone's used to that by now. Apart from the English, mind you; they always look so scared when they turn up on their bikes! Hehehe. But I'm originally from Cameroon.'

They carried on talking for a good quarter of an hour, and even though George was starting to feel exhausted, he was grateful to this man for keeping him company. And it wasn't every day he got to speak to someone from Cameroon.

He finally plucked up the courage to ask the question that had been on his mind since they had started talking.

'Listen, this might seem, well … I guess it's complicated. I was wondering if … if … if you could possibly take my mobile phone with you when you leave and read my text messages in the car park, just to see if there's anything urgent on there, you see. And then you can tell me what's in them tomorrow, or whenever you have time. But only if it's not too much trouble, of course.'

'It's no trouble at all! But if you'd prefer, I can go down to the car park now, and come back when I've read them. I'll take notes if there are a lot of them. My memory's not what it used to be.'

He put his large, wrinkled hand into his breast pocket and pulled out his reading glasses, a little orange notebook and a pencil that had been sharpened so much that it was nothing more than a little stub. George smiled; he had one just the same in his overalls at home.

George carefully explained to him how the phone worked and how to access his voicemails. The man took careful notes.

'Alright, I'll be back in five minutes.'

A few moments later, a nurse came in to prepare him for bed, and George was reminded of the injuries he had managed to forget. Five minutes later, the hospital worker reappeared, brandishing his notebook.

'You've got mail!' he said, chuckling.

He put his glasses on, opened his notebook and began to read very solemnly, like a parishioner reading a psalm at mass.

'You got four texts. The first one is from Ginette Bruneau, it says: 'The sun is out again, I had lunch out on the terrace with a friend and thought of your visit in September. I hope the weather will still be good when you come back. Love to both of you, take care of yourselves.' The second and third ones are from Adèle, and I think it's better if you just read what I've written down, because they're in some kind of shorthand, and I don't ... Well, anyway I copied everything out word for word.'

1. Adèle

Shoot almst ova, we r workin even hrder now, even on w/e. im thinkin bout goin away in nov if i dnt get mor (paid!) wrk. But til then iv got no time. How was chato CelleG?

(Shooting almost over, we are working even harder now, even on the weekend. I am thinking about going away in November if I don't get more (paid!) work. But until then I've got no time. How was Château La Celle-Guenand?)

2. Adèle

Hvnt hrd frm u. U OK?

(I haven't heard from you. You OK?)

'And in the fourth one, which was also from Ginette, there was no message, just a photo. An MMS I think you call it.'

'A photo? I've never had one of them before. A photo of what?'

'The sea.'

The two men said nothing for a while. George sighed. He didn't know where Charles was, he didn't know whether to tell Adèle or not. She had better things to do than to trek out to the middle of nowhere to see her grandfather. What should he reply? Could he ask this man to reply for him?

'I can reply to your ladies, if you like,' said the hospital worker before George had time to decide what he wanted. 'When I go home.'

'Oh, well if you could ... But I'm not sure what I want to say to them.'

George explained to his new friend who these ladies were and told him all about the Tour de France.

'The Tour de France?'

'Yes, but not on a bike, right?'

'Yeah, I'd guessed that much with your legs,' he chuckled. 'But even so, three thousand five hundred kilometres in a car? That's some journey! You'll be heading to the south then? My wife and I have always wanted to visit the south – Saint-Tropez, right? Actually no, Saint-Tropez probably isn't as good as all that, and it's not really for the likes of us, is it? But the Tour went through Nîmes, didn't it?'

'Stage thirteen, Narbonne–Nîmes.'

'And then to Digne-les-Bains, I remember seeing them on telly.'

One thing led to another and before they knew it, the two men had been talking for over an hour.

'So, have you decided what you're going to say to these ladies?'

George's face clouded over. After a moment's reflection he made some careful notes in the notebook and handed it back to the hospital worker, who read them in silence before putting the pencil, notebook and phone in his pocket.

'OK, so I'll keep the phone for tonight, and if you never see me again, it'll be 'cause I've sold it on eBay and run off to Saint-Tropez, right?' He burst out laughing again. 'Just kidding! Ask for George.'

'That's my name too,' said George.

'Well, there you go! Great minds think alike; no, great Georges think alike!' Another peal of high-pitched laughter.

And he walked away laughing. A few minutes later the doctor walked in with bad news. They would have to operate in three days' time. General anaesthetic.

Monday 13 October

Loches (Indre-et-Loire)

Charles gently opened the door, and George was hit by a wave of sadness. He couldn't shake the feeling that by stopping now he was betraying his friend. He smiled weakly at him.

'Charles.'

'We came yesterday, but you were pretty out of it.'

'Who's we?'

'Thérèse and I.'

'Oh, Thérèse … So she came all the way here? She's a good friend. But how are you doing, Charles?'

'I'm fine.'

'I'm sort of abandoning you, aren't I?'

'No, no, not at all.'

'Yes, I am, and I don't know what I can do about it. You know I'd love to keep going, if only for your sake …'

George had tears in his eyes; Charles couldn't meet his gaze. Instead, he made do with patting him on the arm.

'They're going to operate on me, so ...' said George in a whisper. 'All those years we were neighbours ... They were good years, you know.'

George stopped, unable to continue, but Charles knew what he was trying to say.

'Of course, there were a few ups and downs along the way,' George added.

'Oh sure, but on the whole ...'

'Yes, on the whole ...' George nodded slowly. 'So what are you going to do?'

'Well, that's actually why Thérèse is here. Quite a lot has happened over the last few days, so I might as well start at the beginning. Firstly, I've spoken to some of the doctors here. This whole Tour thing ... I'm not saying it's a miracle cure, but it really is helping, George, I can feel it. And the doctors agree. And Thérèse can see it as well. Nothing gets past her, you know. And she can tell it's working. I mean, of course, when I told her you'd had an accident she didn't think twice before coming here. We've been talking a lot, and we were thinking, if you're not game any more ...'

'Oh,' sighed George. 'It's not that I'm not game, old chap, it's my body that's given up ... And then there's that lot ...' He gestured towards the corridor, where the nurses were hurrying about their work.

'Alright, well, we'll see,' Charles said. 'But anyway ... what was I going to say ...? Oh yes! We were at the Volkswagen dealer this morning … and we've bought ourselves a camper van. It's got everything we need in it. We're going travelling!'

'A camper van? Charles!' exclaimed George, grinning. 'And you're really going to travel around in it? How long are you going away for?'

'As long as it takes. We'll probably put the house up for sale. And Marcel, you remember Marcel from Erquy, the guy who went swimming every day?'

'Oh yes, of course, Marcel.'

'Right, well, Marcel and his wife might come with us.'

George didn't know what to say. He thought it was a marvellous idea. Finally, he asked:

'And Thérèse is happy to come along? She won't mind leaving her dahlias and chickens for such a long time?'

'It was her idea, George.'

They fell silent again, each man smiling to himself. George felt his eyes welling up again, but this time they were not tears of sadness.

'I'd better get going. Thérèse is off buying the provisions, but we'll come back to see you tomorrow morning. I'll bring the brochure for the camper van. When is your operation?'

'The day after tomorrow.'

'Have you called Françoise?'

'I've asked the doctors to try to get hold of her, wherever she is at the moment.'

'And you're sure they'll find her?'

'Oh yes, they'll track her down somehow. Email and all that. Right, Charles. Go and help Thérèse, and give her my love.

You're lucky, you know, Charles, to have a wife like that.'

'I know, I know.'

Just as Charles was about to leave, George remembered something important:

'Listen, if I do kick the bucket ... I want you to write the inscription on my gravestone ... in pig Latin!'

Charles smiled, told him not to be ridiculous, and left.

Once again, George was all alone in his room. He was still in pain, but he felt as though a weight had been lifted from his chest. Outside, the wind chased after the swirling autumn leaves. His room telephone rang. George let it ring a few times before he picked up.

'Dad? It's me.'

Tuesday 14 October

Loches (Indre-et-Loire)

In the corridor, Adèle passed a black hospital worker who smiled at her, but all her attention was fixed on the room numbers and she didn't see him. She finally found number 412, gave a tiny knock on the door, and walked in as quietly as possible. She was afraid; afraid that she would not have the courage to face her grandfather's suffering, afraid that she would not prove a worthy granddaughter to this man who might not survive the night. She saw her grandfather and was struck by how old he looked. And much thinner than in the photos her mother had shown her. But she also saw that he recognised her, and that his eyes had filled with tears.

She wished she could erase all the years she had been absent, and do something, anything useful and generous. But even stronger than that was the urge to flee, so she wouldn't have to say any of the things she had prepared in her head. In the space of a few days, she had begun to get to know her grandfather; now long-buried memories were starting to float to the surface of her mind. Nothing tangible, nothing she could have put into words, no precise images, just outlines, just the vague feeling that she had once been a child, that she was no longer a child, and that she and her grandfather had had some good times together, once.

He was happy to see her; he seemed at peace. He took her hands in his, which were surprisingly soft.

'How are you, how was the journey?'

'Oh fine, it's actually not that far, you know,' lied Adèle.

'That's good,' said George, holding her gaze. 'I'm so glad you came, you didn't have to – and your bosses weren't angry with you for missing a few days?'

'Oh no, I'll go back this evening. But how are you, Grandpa?'

'Fine, I'm fine. Don't think I'll be around for much longer, you know.'

Adèle didn't know how to react to this.

'You mustn't say that, Grandpa, you'll get better. I bet you'll be up and about in no time.'

Her grandfather said nothing, and stared down at his hands. After a moment he looked up at her and said:

'It really means a lot to me that you came, sweetheart. It really does.'

Neither of them knew what to say after this. Adèle, unable to bear the silence, said:

'Oh, you have a television in your room, that's good. Are you comfortable here?'

'You know, Adèle … There's something I've been thinking about a lot over the past few days.' He paused for a moment, and looked around the room, before looking back down at his hands, clasped in his lap.

'Do you remember the time when you, your grandmother and I went to see the nativity scene in Bressuire?'

Adèle could indeed picture the sight of the brightly lit manger that had seemed so huge and majestic that it had looked like a whole town to her, illuminated by thousands of tiny lights – it had been magical. This was a very old memory.

'You know, I think about that day a lot.'

'It was a lovely evening.'

'When we all got home, you refused to go to sleep; the whole thing had made you far too overexcited. You must have been about eight or nine years old, no more than that. And at the time, we were more than a little worried about your grandmother's health, and I wasn't in great shape either. It wasn't that we were unhappy, your grandmother and I, but ... let's just say it was a difficult patch. And your parents had their own things to be getting on with; it was the holidays and we were always happy to have you with us, sweetheart. But your grandmother and I were both exhausted. And you know I had an angry streak back then. Oh, these things fade with time, you know, that's just the way life goes. But at the time it wasn't a good idea to get on my bad side. Anyway, where was I ...? Oh yes, on that day, we came home from the nativity and you were very overexcited. Do you remember, you just wouldn't go to bed, jumping up and down on the bed? There was no stopping you. Your grandmother tried to get you down from the bed as you were jumping so you pulled her hair. And I just lost it.'

He paused again.

'I grabbed you and smacked you so hard it left a red mark on your bottom.'

Adèle smiled. She could remember the nativity scene, but not the smack. She looked at her grandfather, laughing.

'Well, I'm sure I deserved it, I know I was a little difficult at that age!'

She realised this was the end of the story. Her grandfather put his head in his hands.

'Oh sweetheart, I was so angry with myself at the time. I was younger then, and I'd like to think I've changed since, but I never forgave myself. And the older I get, the more I regret that evening.'

'But Grandpa, I can't even remember it, I promise!'

'After that you stopped coming so often, and then when you were a teenager you barely came to see us at all. And whenever I thought about it, I was reminded of that evening after the nativity. In our day, you see, we were always smacked when we'd been bad …'

He carried on; Adèle let him speak. He also clearly felt guilty about the long silence between them. He also blamed himself for it. How could she tell him that it had nothing to do with that unfortunate incident, which she couldn't even remember? Still, it would have been a simple explanation for ten years of silence – a little thing that could be dated, analysed and categorised, where there was a perpetrator and a victim. It would have left nothing for the psychiatrists, everything could have been resolved, the angry blow forgiven and everyone would live happily ever after.

But was this true? No, of course it wasn't. The real reason was much more difficult to express. Adèle finally interrupted him and took his hand.

'Grandpa, I really don't remember you smacking me, I promise I don't. I remember the figures in the manger and twinkling lights everywhere, I remember being enchanted by the whole thing. But you smacking me ...'

Her grandfather looked at her but did not reply.

He could have said, as Irving Ferns might have: 'How time passes, my dear. We old people know how it goes. Time takes our friends from us, puts our grandchildren at a distance and plays tricks on our memories. And all the while you young people know nothing of time, you're all invincible, always on the go, always out of reach.' But this was no time for grievances. He had wanted to apologise for what he had done. And now he had.

Now it was Adèle's turn. And she wanted to tell the story of Irving Ferns.

Tuesday 16 September

London

Irving Ferns had been cast primarily because of his physique. In the novel, Agatha Christie had described the character, eighty-three-year-old Aristide Leonides, as a small, ugly man who nevertheless possessed an irresistible charm that women seemed to find incredibly attractive – in other words, a complete nightmare for even the most talented casting director. It turned out that Mr Ferns was about the same age, and happened also to be small and very ugly. As for irresistible charm, his sixty-year career in film and theatre would see to that. Irving, as he was known in the business, had enjoyed a respectable career both on screen and on stage, but since turning sixty he had had to make do with minor television roles in exchange for pitiable fees. This perhaps explained the vivid impression he had made on Adèle when she had first accompanied him from his taxi to the set: everything about Irving Ferns, his eyes, his mannerisms, his whole body, seemed to be apologising for not being younger; he seemed to be desperately and silently fighting off the indecent advances of old age. But in vain: Adèle knew that his age would make him an outsider amongst his younger colleagues. When she saw he had difficulty walking, she offered him her arm. Initially they simply exchanged small talk, and as they covered all the usual pleasantries, Adèle decided that this man probably lived alone. The collar of his shirt was too big and his thin neck resembled that of a chicken. Having lost contact with her grandparents, Adèle, like most cosmopolitan young people, barely came into contact with 'the elderly'. There were no elderly people in London: had they all left or had they been forced to leave? The streets of the city belonged to the young: to the yuppies, City boys, It girls and yummy mummies, second-generation immigrants and those who had just arrived – all of these people were young. Talking to Irving Ferns was like talking to a character in a novel. Yet just as she was about to start feeling really sorry for him, Irving Ferns surprised her by changing the subject from the weather to something altogether different.

Gradually a connection formed between them. Irving must have known that it was Adèle's job to keep him happy, but he took this as an opportunity to engage her in conversation. Adèle had won him over with her natural warmth, and it was not long before he opened up to her as a friend. Although timid at first, the tone of the conversation became more and more lively, and after a while their age difference, far from being an obstacle, became a distance that, paradoxically, seemed to make them even more at ease with one another. Whether in the green room, on set or in the cafeteria, they always found something to talk about.

Irving told her a lot about his past, and Adèle had to admit that it was a fascinating story. He had worked with some of the greats of British cinema and had, like many actors of his era, been a great fan of the practical joke, and of farce comedy. He also told her about his on-screen love affairs, his successes and his failures. Adèle found his stories funny and moving, and she began to see Irving as he had once been: an up-and-coming actor, a cultivated dandy, and a romantic at heart. He began to feel young again in front of Adèle, his newly captivated audience.

Wednesday 17 September

London

On the second day of shooting, Irving sought out Adèle in the canteen at lunchtime. She was more than happy to sit with him and escape the chattering of the other girls. This time, he paused occasionally in his monologue to ask the young girl about her life: where was her family from, how long had she been living in London, and so on and so forth. France and the French became, amongst others, a subject to which they regularly returned. Irving's brother, who had been dead for some time, had survived Dunkirk. He remembered the letters from him, and the stories he had told him after the war. He did not, however, turn this story into a tragic tale of a family separated by the war, choosing instead to recount the more comic aspects, something for which Adèle was extremely grateful. She even managed to forget the stress of the first days of shooting. She found herself opening up about her childhood, her plans for the future, her thoughts on her native country and her career, and many more things besides.

After she had refused a sticky slice of sponge drowned in custard, Irving asked her if her grandparents were still alive. She said yes, she had a grandfather who lived in the French countryside. Did she visit him often? No, in fact she had barely spoken to him in ten years. She had seen a lot of him when she was younger, but you know how it is, people lose touch with one another and then, well …

Irving looked at her carefully. Yes, Irving knew. And he knew what came after the 'and then' that Adèle had left unsaid. Indifference.

Irving Ferns left the set having shot his last scene. Adèle had continued to escort him between the dressing rooms and the set but it was as though the heart-to-heart of the previous evening had never happened. Irving was as polite as ever, of course, but nothing more; the note of complicity in his voice had vanished. Anyone else would have assumed that he was simply in a mood. Actors were known for being rather volatile in this respect – even Adèle, who was just beginning, knew that. After all, they were carrying all kinds of characters around in their heads and were often under immense pressure. But Adèle couldn't help but wonder. Perhaps Irving Ferns had been disappointed in her. Perhaps he had thought that she wasn't the type to forget about her grandfather.

Irving Ferns had awoken an old feeling of guilt that had lain dormant for a long time, and which weighed a little more on her conscience with each birthday that went by. Every time she thought about it, she would tell herself … What did she tell herself? Nothing at all, because there was nothing to say about it. She just tried not to think about it. She was almost twenty-three, she ought to have outgrown her selfish, capricious teenage nature. Why hadn't she contacted her grandfather for so long? Was she secretly harbouring bad memories of the holidays she had spent with him? No, Adèle had always mistaken what was in fact a very happy childhood for a boring one. She had no regrets, no grudges, no skeletons in her closet. Had her grandfather been a fairy-tale villain? No. Had he held extreme political opinions, had friends in the wrong places or a dark past? No, not as far as she knew. And yet she had grown so far apart from him that when she spoke about him, she did so in the past tense. He wasn't dead. Not yet. He had had health problems in the past, of course, and the death of his wife had been a grave blow. He had lived alone for so many years and still, still Adèle had not made any effort with him.

That night Adèle turned her conversation with the actor over and over in her mind, and kept coming back to her unfinished sentence. In the darkness she felt her grandfather's loneliness just as she had sensed that of Irving Ferns. And although she had been able to empathise with an elderly actor she had known for a couple of days, she had not been able to do the same for her grandfather, the man with whom she had spent all of her childhood holidays. Suddenly, she felt ashamed of herself and fell asleep resolving to call her grandfather the very next day.

Tuesday 14 October

Loches (Indre-et-Loire)

And that was the story of her and Irving Ferns. Without dramatic declarations, without shocking revelations, without pearls of wisdom or pomposity, the old man had helped Adèle take this decisive step that had changed so much over the past few weeks. And now she had to tell her grandfather the story.

Adèle gathered all her courage and began talking, her voice trembling slightly.

'You remember, Grandpa, I told you I was working on a film about the murder of an old millionnaire. And on the first day we filmed the scene … the scene where the body is found.'

'Oh sweetheart, and that made you think of your old grandpa lying there in his place? Murdered! Well, that would be something wouldn't it?' he said jokingly.

'Oh no, the whole thing is so staged, and there are spotlights everywhere, and wigs and stuff dangling all over the place, and the crew all around you; it's pretty hard to lose yourself in the scene. And I couldn't see much of the action anyway, so ... But the man who was playing the part was about your age. And ... I ended up getting on pretty well with him.'

She paused for a moment to steady her voice, which was becoming increasingly shaky.

'And because I got on so well with him, I thought to myself, there's no reason why I wouldn't get on just as well with you. I think when you're young, and a teenager and all that, you forget that you can still be friends with your granddad, you know.'

She stopped talking. Her grandfather looked at her encouragingly.

'You're right, sweetheart. I felt the same way. When you're old, you forget that you can still relate to young people.' He laughed. 'We're a right pair, aren't we?'

He sniffed, then took his granddaughter's hand.

'You know, Adèle, people always say that life is too short. But for so long, for *so* long, I thought that it felt too long. But now ... I'm starting to think it's been exactly right.'

George-from-Cameroon spent a lot of time in George-from-Chanteloup's bedroom. He came to see him after Adèle had left, and found the old man looking a little shaken.

That evening they talked for a long time – or, for as long as the coming and going of the nurses and doctors allowed them to – and carried on well after visiting hours were over. At first, George-from-Chanteloup was the one speaking, with George-from-Cameroon chiming in with the niceties that have always accompanied great friendships. 'You're always your own worst enemy'; 'It's just like with family reunions; better to leave while you're still having fun, so you keep the best memories.'

But sometimes, George-from-Cameroon spoke more, and George listened carefully; talking things over with his new companion made everything seem simpler. They discussed the moving phone conversation with Françoise, and what she had told him. The small, crumpled orange notebook was brought out, scribbled on, put back, brought out again, consulted, scribbled on again, inspected, put away and brought out and put away again. Every now and again they would stop talking for a moment and just listen to the sounds of the hospital. Their voices grew quieter as the conversation went on, so that by the time they said goodnight they were almost whispering. George thought about this conversation and what had been said, and wrote letters to Charles, to Adèle, to Françoise, and to Ginette. Would this be enough? Was it ever enough?

By this time it was already getting light. It was the morning of the operation.

Wednesday 15 October

Loches (Indre-et-Loire)

George was taken to the operating room. Was he scared? Worried? No; never before had he felt so profoundly himself. He was an island, a huge island made of everything he had been and had ever dreamed of being: all of his memories, the feelings he had never been able to control, the body that had been the cause of so much joy, pain, strength and despair. All of the things that made George Nicoleau who he was were on this island, on this hospital bed.

On the operating table this feeling momentarily disappeared, and he felt the island breaking up, scattering. But the sight of the other George, George-from-Cameroon, smiling at him from a corner of the room, helped him gather his strength. He was put under anaesthetic, which made him feel as though he were floating on gently undulating waves. George-from-Cameroon was still smiling; so was George-from-Chanteloup, even if no one could see it.

Saturday 18 October

Poitiers (Vienne)

The news did not come as a surprise to anyone except the doctors. They had gone over percentages, medication, emergency measures, had listed everything they had and had not been able to do. George had never regained consciousness.

Adèle had not been able to get back before now. The funeral had been planned for the next day. Her mother, who had just arrived from Peru, would be waiting for her at Poitiers airport. She had not been able to make it back in time to say goodbye to her father, which broke Adèle's heart.

Adèle stepped onto the tarmac, her eyes fixed firmly on the ground. She didn't dare look up at the tiny airport; she had not seen her mother for almost two months. She was afraid of telling her the whole story, she was afraid of grief, of her own and her mother's. She was overwhelmed by the events of the last few days.

Finally, she caught sight of her mother. The woman who normally had perfect posture, whose stylish suits hung elegantly on her slim frame, was now wearing jeans and a dark jumper and was sitting alone on a bench in the deserted terminal. They hugged, holding on to each other for a long time, both trying, in vain, not to cry. It was her mother who finally pulled away, looking at Adèle with a smile.

'You look like you've lost weight,' she said.

'It's the food on set,' replied Adèle, wiping her eyes with her sleeve. 'It's horrible, the stuff they serve us, full of sugar and fat. So I just don't eat it. When did you get here?'

'Yesterday evening.'

'How was the trek?'

'I didn't go on a trek,' Françoise answered, sounding oddly calm.

'Oh? Was it cancelled or something?'

'No. There never was any trek. Oh, I was in Peru, but in Lima. I had a phone, internet, email, even my mobile worked out there. I had everything.'

'Oh. Well Grandpa thought that—'

'Yes, I know. I spoke to him on the phone on Monday. I told him everything. He understood.'

Adèle felt a surge of anger. She had never liked lies and she was not sure what to make of this one. They were now the only ones in the terminal, which seemed vast, in the middle of the empty airport. There wouldn't be another plane here until the evening.

Adèle tugged awkwardly at her sleeves until her mother spoke again.

'You know, Adèle, your grandfather was ill for a very long time. For about fifteen years, actually. And for the last five years, since your grandmother died, I was the one who looked after him. I was all he had; I couldn't just give up on him, and I was doing it all on my own. You know he never wanted a nurse or anything. For five years I was constantly in contact with his doctors, constantly making sure his affairs were in order "just in case"; basically holding him up, all that time. So many times I kissed him for what I thought was the last time. So many times I came running back when I thought it was the end. And things have changed in my life over the past five years, with your father, you know, even after the divorce, things were difficult, and then I met Patrick just as Grandpa got very ill again, seriously ill with his ulcers, you probably don't remember. I ended up spending more time looking after him than living my own life, or ... Anyway, that's how it was.'

She paused for a moment before continuing.

'And then one day last year, I realised that I had to make a choice, because it couldn't go on like that.' Her voice was steady, but Adèle could hear a note of fragility that she had never heard before. Shyly, she tried to take her mother's hand, but Françoise gently pulled it back.

'I'll spare you the details, sweetheart, especially because everything is much better now, I promise. But I had to start taking care of myself. And by talking to friends who've been through similar things, and then to a psychologist ... I've realised a lot of things.'

She stopped talking, and took a deep breath. Adèle looked at her mother, and noticed she looked more tired than normal, and older.

'I had to let your grandpa live his life. Even if that meant letting him go – I mean literally letting him go – because that was what he wanted. And I had a life to live as well. We were so unhappy together. I was too attached to him; I would have preserved him in formaldehyde if I could have, he said. And he was probably right. We both needed some fresh air. I talked to Thérèse a lot about all of this, and she told me about what Charles was going through. One day she told me about their Tour de France plan, and what she hoped it would do for Charles. I knew how much your grandfather was looking forward to it, because it was a way out, even if he knew he was taking huge risks with his health. But if I had still been on the scene, he would never have gone. So I decided that it was now or never. I went to Lima to stay with a friend and have some time alone. But it wasn't an easy decision. I asked Thérèse to keep me in the loop. She called me when he was taken to hospital but I … I didn't come back straight away. It wasn't the first time your grandfather had been taken to hospital, you know … And in some way, maybe we had already said our goodbyes.'

Françoise put her head in her hands. Her shoulders were shaking slightly. Adèle put her arms around her mother. She was no longer angry. The sun cast huge shadows through the terminal windows. The storm had passed.

When it started to rain again an hour later, the terminal was filled with their laughter. The Tour, which had had such an impact on their little family, was a mine of anecdotes that Adèle took great pleasure in exaggerating for the amusement of her mother. By retelling all the stories with the help of her mobile phone, she was able to prove to her mother that she had made the right decision.

They finally left the airport and drove a hire car to the Grand Hôtel de Poitiers, where Françoise, in an effort to put off the inevitable task of going to her father's empty house, had reserved two rooms.

It was there that she would have to summon the courage to open a package wrapped in brown paper that had been sent to her by someone called George N'Dour, along with two letters.

Françoise took a deep breath and ripped open the paper to find an old wooden box with a faded picture of the *Pieds Nickelés* comic book characters on the lid. She had a vague memory of it belonging to her when she was a child. Her throat tightened and her heart was pounding as she worked up the courage to open it. She pulled it open as quickly as possible, as though ripping off a plaster. The box was empty.

She examined the inside for a hidden compartment but found nothing. Then, bit by bit, the real story behind the box came back to her. The box hadn't been hers; it had belonged to her cousin. How had her father got hold of it? Perhaps the letters would explain.

Her name had been written carefully in ink on one of the envelopes, with a note beneath it scrawled in pencil: 'Read this one first.' She opened the envelope and pulled out an elegant sheet of writing paper.

Chanteloup, 16 September

Dear Françoise,

I'm setting off with Charles on the Tour de France because I can't bear the thought of wasting away in my armchair. I hope with all my heart that you can forgive me for leaving you. I wasn't brave enough to talk to you about this. One word from you would have been enough to make me stay; I miss you.

When you were a little girl, you always said that this box was the most beautiful thing you'd ever seen, but at the time your mother and I weren't able to buy you one. I found this one on the internet (eBay) and I thought it would make you smile.

I couldn't have asked for a better daughter. Take good care of yourself.

Papa

Françoise sat on the bed holding the letter for a long time, her heart heavy. She reread it, smiling at the word 'eBay', but she soon felt tears running down her face again. The second letter had been written hastily in pencil on several sheets of squared paper that looked as though they had been torn out of a notebook.

14/10/2008

Dear Françoise,
Since I wrote the letter you have just read, a lot has happened in my life, much of it unexpected. I have discovered a new favourite region: Brittany! Adèle has told me she will try to go there on holiday, I hope you'll be able to go with her. I have recently seen Ginette again (Charles's sister, who remembers you). She is a wonderful woman and someone I care for very much. She'd be very happy if you visited

her one day; her address is 14 Passage des Pêcheurs, 85690 Notre-Dame-de-Monts, where she has a very lovely house. George N'Dour, who sent you this letter, is one of the many friends I have made along the way on this trip. Please keep in touch with Charles and Thérèse as well, who are going to sell their house and go travelling. The Tour has also shown me how much I have underestimated my neighbour Charles for the last thirty years. He is a brave and generous friend, who knows a lot more about the world than he lets on. This goes for Thérèse too. I am leaving them the Renault (you must remind the notary). Promise me to keep an eye on them, and to lend them a hand if they ever get in a tight spot money-wise.

Lastly, this has been a chance to get to know my granddaughter again. Adèle is a remarkable young woman. She has made me a very proud grandfather. She will be able to tell you about all of our adventures in detail, because we wrote to each other a lot during the trip, and she knows all there is to know. I made her promise to tell her grandchildren about our journey! I hope that you will take good care of yourself. You have given me so much over the last few years, and I will never be able to thank you enough. All my affairs are in order (thanks to you!), so don't worry about that. As for me, I'm going out on a high note. Because it's like with family reunions; better to leave while you're still having fun, so you keep the best memories.

All my love,
Your father.

All was silent in Françoise's room, in the hotel, in the street, in the town. There was nothing left to say.

Sunday 19 October

Chanteloup (Deux-Sèvres)

It did not take long to organise the funeral. Françoise and her father had had it all planned for a long time, and her father had been very precise about what he wanted. Later, Adèle would remember certain details about the ceremony: the grey marble that perfectly matched the sky, the plastic flowers, the wicker chairs in the church, her shoes crunching in the gravel in the cemetery, the unfamiliar faces gathering around his grave. Just like at any other funeral. She had not felt at ease.

It was the morning before the funeral that she would remember the best. She and her mother were at her grandfather's house getting changed. In the house next door, Charles and Thérèse were also getting ready. Adèle had barely had time to walk around the village she had not seen for ten years. All of her attention was focused on her mother, who was trying to hold back tears. Even now, Françoise was as elegant and well turned out as ever. Adèle went downstairs to make coffee in the kitchen.

The house still felt lived in. Her grandparents' house, that she thought she had forgotten. How wrong she was.

Everything came back to her in a powerful wave of memory. She was amazed to find that she still remembered where they kept the coffee cups, the tea towels, and the instant coffee. And the porcelain pot where her grandmother had hidden her secret supply of marshmallows. The soup tureen on the sideboard where her grandfather had kept his receipts. The pencil drawer. She remembered the garden, which could be seen from the window above the sink – it was much smaller than she remembered, of course, but she recognised all the trees, the rocks, the lilacs, the pond at the end of the garden, and the blue ropes that formed a barrier around it. As she looked around the room, happy, colourful memories appeared from every corner. All the little trinkets in the house suddenly became precious; she would have liked to keep every last one of them, like rare flowers or butterflies on a pinboard. But could she preserve the familiar smell of the cupboard where they kept the board games or the taste of the toffees that came back to her when she saw the blue sweet box? Or her grandfather's careful handwriting on the cheques she received from him on her birthday? She knew it would have made her grandfather smile to see her reminiscing like this. She had to repress the urge to send him a text message. Before she had time to be sad that this was no longer possible, she caught sight of something that caused yet more childhood memories to come rushing back like an incoming tide. It was a photo of her mother as a little girl in a pretty handmade frame that reminded Adèle of being pushed around outside in a wheelbarrow overflowing with hay. A reproduction of Van Gogh's *Sunflowers* in the hall brought back the taste of orange blossom that her grandmother used to give her in a glass of water before bedtime. Colourful stacks of paperback books reminded her of endless rounds of Pope Joan where she was always allowed to win. The Duralex glasses in the kitchen represented the bunches of primroses she would bring to her grandmother from the neighbours' field. And there were countless others, memories returned to her in a never-ending flow of images, words, smells, arguments and peals of laughter, every Christmas and Easter, children's games, scraped knees and her grandparents' smiling faces. Before she knew it, hot tears were streaming down her face as they had done when she was a little girl staying in this same house.

It was in the little kitchen that Adèle mourned for her grandfather; not in the cemetery, and not before the marble plaque that would later be put up in his memory. Adèle paid her respects to him in his own house, and bestowed upon him an honour that would have meant more to him than any medal: pride of place in her memories of a very happy childhood.

Tuesday 21 October

London

At last, at the end of the eighth take, they managed to get the scene perfect, and the director called it a wrap. 'Cut! That's it! It's a wrap, ladies and gents!' The whole team burst into applause, there were hugs and cries of congratulation, even a few tears, probably due to tiredness rather than joy. The executive producer, David Lerner, a tall, lanky blond figure who was pushing fifty but still dressed like a Cambridge student, turned up as if by magic and announced that everyone was to join him down in the basement once the set had been cleared. As always, Adèle was the last person to leave the set, having checked that everything was in order, nothing important had been left behind, and everything in the old house was back in its rightful place. She checked every floor, walking down all the corridors with their creaking floorboards, checking behind all the doors. This place almost felt like home, after a month spent in these musty rooms. Her spirits were high, and her mind was still buzzing: not only was the shoot over, she had plans afoot and the future was looking up, but she had just received this seemingly impossible text from her grandfather, and it had given her a lift.

By the time she got down to the basement, the party had already started. There was champagne and cheap canapés going around and the room was filled with laughter. Adèle made her way through the throng and managed to get herself a glass of champagne. She didn't notice the producer, the production manager and her assistants whispering about something in a corner of the room. Suddenly the producer's voice was heard asking for silence.

'Excuse me everybody ... Excuse me! OK, thanks. I'd just like to say a few words. I want to say a huge thank you to all the cast and crew for your excellent work. I've seen the rushes and it looks fabulous. We had a viewing with the head of the channel and she's over the moon as well. I am so proud to have been a part of this film, which I am sure will be a huge success. So thank you all for your excellent work. Cheers!'

'Cheers!' chorused the crowd in reply, applauding enthusiastically. The producer raised his voice again over all the commotion.

'One more thing, one more thing, and then you can start drinking again. OK, we also have a birthday to celebrate today!' The assistants brought out a cake with a candle in it.

'Adèle, where's Adèle? Ah, there she is, there's our Adèle!' And everyone broke into a round of 'Happy Birthday'.

It took Adèle a few moments to realise they were talking about her. She blushed as she blew out the candle. Once again, the producer cut short the applause.

'So, before Adèle makes her speech – don't think you're getting away without one, Adèle – I'd like to say thank you not only to the birthday girl, but also to all of our runners and assistants who have probably worked harder than anyone else here. On set, I am sure all of you noticed that we have several highly qualified assistants' (at this point, several of the more important crew members nodded in agreement) 'and I would like to tell them that they've done a remarkable job, and I say remarkable because I know – having been in that position myself – that they think we don't notice them at all. So, guys, you should know that you have been noticed, and believe me, even if the tasks seem menial at times, I'm telling you that your work is essential, vital to the shoot. So I wish Adèle and all of our runners the very best of luck in their careers in television and cinema. Cheers! And now I'm going to hand you over to our birthday girl.'

Adèle was shaking her head and trying to step back but the producer insisted, clearly in a mischievous mood.

Adèle was still bright red. She hated giving speeches, but it looked as though there was no way out of this one.

'Thank you, thank you very much, David. Um, for those of you who don't know me, I was the crashing noise in the middle of the fourth take. I dropped my phone, but, um, not because I'm clumsy. Something unbelievable had just happened and it was shock that made me drop my phone. You see, I'd got a text from my grandfather wishing me a happy birthday. The thing is, though, I went to his funeral last weekend.'

The crowd suddenly fell totally silent. There were a few nervous laughs. Adèle felt very uncomfortable standing in front of the silent room.

'Well, it sounds a bit morbid, but it actually made me really happy. I mean, after the shock had worn off.'

Alex, who was standing near her, asked the question on everyone's lips: 'How did he do it?' Someone suggested that it was possible to programme phones to send texts at a certain time in the future. Another wondered if it had been a delay with the operator. Maybe someone else had written it for him, or perhaps his phone had been hacked?

When the voices had died down, Adèle said softly:

'Actually, I'd rather not know how it happened. I think my grandfather would have preferred me not to try to work it out.'

And with that, the party resumed; people moved back into their little groups and the mystery text message became the subject of many an animated conversation. Adèle told a good number of the crew about her grandpa's Tour de France, speaking to people she had been deliberately avoiding for the last month. She even told people about her renewed relationship with him, the past mistakes that had been forgiven, the indifference that had kept them apart for years. The ingenuity of the two old men was a particular cause for hilarity. Old people were not at all like you assumed they were! The actor who had replaced Irving Ferns at such short notice nodded firmly in agreement. All around the room, people were recalling family memories, musing on the state of their health, telling anecdotes from the days before the war. Never before had people at a wrap party talked so little about film and so much about grandparents.

The following week, phones were ringing in retirement homes across England and even Poland, Scotland and Italy, and happy, timid voices spoke to one another for the first time in years. But Adèle had no idea.

One year later, on 21 October, Adèle received another birthday text message from her grandfather. And on her next birthday, and the one after that. She never tried to work out where they were coming from.

But every year, on 25 September, she would send him the same text:

In memory of the Tour. All my luv, ur Adl.